JOE BEAUCHEMIN'S STORYTELLER TALES

Joseph Beauchemin

PublishAmerica
Baltimore

© 2010 by Joseph Beauchemin.
All rights reserved. No part of this book may be reproduced, stored in a retrieval system or transmitted in any form or by any means without the prior written permission of the publishers, except by a reviewer who may quote brief passages in a review to be printed in a newspaper, magazine or journal.

First printing

All characters in this book are fictitious, and any resemblance to real persons, living or dead, is coincidental.

PublishAmerica has allowed this work to remain exactly as the author intended, verbatim, without editorial input.

Hardcover 978-1-4512-7295-6
Softcover 978-1-4512-7296-3
PUBLISHED BY PUBLISHAMERICA, LLLP
www.publishamerica.com
Baltimore

Printed in the United States of America

I wish to dedicate this, my third book to all the readers of my last two books. Their support has encouraged me to write this third book "A Story Teller's Tales".

I also want to commend the staff and management of Publish America for the excellent work in publishing my last two books.

Joseph Beauchemin, Author

INTRODUCTION

Welcome to my third book! This book contains a random selection of short stories that I know you will enjoy. Most are fiction but a few are non-fiction based on some of my real life experiences.

This book titled "A Story Teller's Tales" was written at my mountain home, a cabin in Branchport, NY, where the surroundings and the atmosphere are serene and inspirational.

My other two books "Up from Adversity" and "A Triad of My Literary Masterpieces" have been published by Publish America in 2006 and 2007. I appreciate and thank all my readers.

Sincerely,
Joseph Beauchemin
2009

TABLE OF CONTENTS

CHAPTER ONE: ADVENTURE

ADVENTURES AT MENTEETH POINT 11
CAMPING IN BRISTOL VALLEY 16
THE FISHING STORY THAT I NEVER TOLD 21
A NIGHT IN THE LONG WINTER 24
A DAY WITHOUT GLORY 26
THE INITIATION OF A MOUNTAIN MAN 28
A TALE OF TWO BOYHOODS 32
PIERRE AND ROBERT ..... FUR TRAPPERS IN THE 17TH
    CENTURY 37
A NIGHT IN THE EARLY AMERICAN WOODS 42
THE DAY WITH A WOLVERINE 46
A HIDDEN JEWEL IN THE ADIRONDACK
    MOUNTAINS 49
TWO BOYS AND A RAFT OF ADVENTURE 52
BUILDING A THREE STORY TREE HOUSE 57
A TREE HOUSE POEM 61

CHAPTER TWO: MEMORIES

CAMPING WITH DAD 65
GRANDMA ON HER CREEPERS 67
REMEMBERING THE ISLAND FRUIT FARM 69
REMEMBERING MR. PURPLE'S FARM LAND 73
SOME HAPPENINGS FROM MY LIFE 75
46 SHEPARD AVE 82
DAD TAUGHT ME HOW TO DRIVE 84

A VISIT TO PINE POND 87
THE HIKE UP THE MOUNTAIN 92
THE CARROT CAKE STORY 95

CHAPTER THREE: INSPIRATIONAL

THE HURRAH FOR THE RUSHVILLE CLINIC 99
MY NEIGHBORS COMPASSIONATE ACT 101
A TREATISE-WORDS OF FAITH 103
JOSEPH BEAUCHEMIN HISTORY 105
HER AFFECTIONATE SMILE 109
OUR MEETING IN FAITH WITH FATHER EDISON 110
THE TRAGIC FALL 111
WHAT MAMA ALWAYS SAID 113
THE LIGHT OF FAITH 114
AN EMERGENCY MOVE TO THE MOUNTAINS 115
BOBBY AND GINNY 118

CHAPTER FOUR: MYSTERY

THE MYSTERY ON THE PENN YAN BLUFF 125
ACCUSATION AND ACQUITAL 128
THE STORY OF LONE EAGLE 132
A MOUNTAIN FAMILY'S TRAGEDY 135

CHAPTER ONE

Adventure

ADVENTURES AT MENTEETH POINT

By Joseph Beauchemin

About eight miles out on the West Lake Road of Canandaigua Lake, there is an impressive twelve-foot high water falls, with a trout stream coming out of the gorge and flowing into Canandaigua Lake. The first time Joe saw the falls, he was on a winter hiking adventure as a Boy Scout. The water flowing over the falls was frozen and the ice had formed in thick strands down the face of the falls. The sunshine on them created prisms of rainbow colors radiating up through the ice. It made such an impression on his memory that remembering the falls inspired him to return again soon.

His first opportunity to return to the falls was in autumn of the next year. At that time of year flies and mosquitoes will be dormant and would not be pestering anyone.

Bobby, Don, Skip and Joe rode their bikes for eight miles to get to Menteeth for a weekend of camping. However, after they arrived, and before they could set up camp, loud noises of thunder, with strong winds, and torrents of rain, threatened to spoil their camping weekend. There is a carriage house there with a roof and dirt floor. One side is open to the outside like a lean-to. Because of the rain, every bit of the ground outdoors is spongy wet and there is no place in the outdoors where they could make a camp. Bobby went to the owner's house to ask him for permission to camp in the carriage house, but the house was dark and appeared deserted. Under the circumstances with no place else to camp, because of the weather conditions, Bobby told the boys to set up their camp in the carriage house. It was considered to be an emergency decision, without permission.

The boys brought their packs and bedrolls inside the carriage house. They started a campfire that made the area warm and dry. They all sat around the fire.

Bobby seemed to be attracted to something outside the lean-to. At first, he questioned what he was seeing, and then he knew what it was! There was someone hiding in those bushes and spying on them.

"All right stranger! Come out of those bushes and get in here by the fire. Tell us who you are, and why you are spying on us!" Bobby demanded.

Then a boy came out of the bushes and came inside and he stood by the fire.

"Who are you? Why were you hiding and spying on the boys?" Bobby asked the boy again.

The stranger said, "My name is John Carr! I have been given the responsibility, by the owner, to watch over this property for him. I saw a fire in the carriage house, and I came here to investigate what caused it. I live in the next house up the road. I was hiding and spying until I found out. Who are you boys and just what are you doing in here, without permission? That's trespassing! You should leave, but seeing that you are already here, and every place is wet, you can stay, with my permission." said John Carr. "Also you can explore and enjoy the falls, if you'd like too. If you climb up the bank on the side of the falls, please be careful because it is always slippery! Be extremely careful with your fires. Also, I'll expect you to clean things up when you leave. You may want to explore the stream above the falls, after things dry out. Fossils and Arrowheads have been found up there. Have a good time, boys!" John said.

In the carriage house Don was making the fire. Skip was quietly checking the dirt floor, seeking the best spot for a bedroll, to claim it for his sleeping spot.

He spread out his bedroll there to get first claim of that spot. Bobby was cooking a meal, for them. Joe was making popcorn for a treat that night. Their supper was hamburgers, potatoes and peaches. They all ate a good meal, and the peaches were great.

After supper that night they all sat around the campfire. Most of them were staring spell bound into the flames as they flickered up and down. Popcorn was brought out and the amounts of each helping made everyone get talkative and smiling again.

Don played his guitar and everyone sang camp songs as they sat cross-legged on the floor around the fire. They ate the rest of the popcorn. It was a good choice for a treat.

A loud "YEOW!" scream shook everyone up. Skip had been examining his hunting knife. He ended up slicing his finger and its bleeding scared him. Bobby applied pressure and got it stopped then he bandaged it.

Bobby said to him, "Put that darn knife away, now! Why were you playing with it, instead of singing with Don and Joe? Get in there, by the fire!" Bobby meant business.

Skip wanted to go looking for something to eat, but saw that Bobby was keeping an eye on him, so he stayed by the fire, singing songs.

As the expression goes, 'boys will be boys', meaning they get into mischief. The sound of someone prowling around, searching for something to eat could be heard. Skip got away from the fire. He was searching for anything that he could find to eat. He smuggled a can of tomato soup that he found somewhere. He brought the can and placed it beside the hot coals of the fire to heat the soup. The bad part was that he didn't poke a hole in the can to let the steam out. Suddenly and unexpectedly, the can burst open and sprayed everyone around the fire with red sticky tomato soup!

"Now clean it all up, quickly and thoroughly, or you will be sleeping outdoors!" Bobby threatened. "Then, get to bed and this time, stay there!

The rest of the campers left the fun by the fire and they went to bed too and shortly after, the camp was quiet, except for the snoring.

The second day at Menteeth that morning looked like it had to be a great day. The rain was over and the sun and wind were doing a great job of drying things out. It will be a fine day for outdoor activities .The boys decided to do some exploring in the stream above the falls, but first they had to climb up that slippery bank on the side of the falls. Bobby went first. He dug his heels in as he climbed up. He always was lucky, and he made it to the top on the first try. He walked over to the edge of the falls. There was a large amount of water flowing over the falls. The water in the stream was high also. Bobby stood there, studying the natural beauty. He took a big stretch and then he went back to the boys at the slippery bank to help others get up.

Joe was next. He did pretty good, but half way up, his foot slipped and he came sliding back down, butt first! He got up and he tried again. This time he made it. That left only Skip and Don. They came up together, side-by-side, helping each other and they made it to the top. They all gathered at the top of the falls by the steam. They hiked upstream for three miles. They saw many good camping sites for future trips. They had a refreshing time hiking in the chilly stream water. They found several interesting fossils and Don uncovered a couple of great looking Arrowheads. On the way coming back to camp, they raced each other down the slippery bank, then waded and swam in the big natural pool at the bottom of the falls.

Back at camp they were serving hot dogs on a stick. They made lemonade to drink. Bobby went next door to see if John Carr would join them. Bobby expressed again how grateful they were to John for letting them camp in the carriage house.

The End

CAMPING IN BRISTOL VALLEY

By Joseph Beauchemin

One gorgeous day in the summer of 1950, two friends, Park and Joe wanted to camp in the beautiful Bristol Valley, about twelve miles from their homes, but first they had to get transportation to the valley. They convinced one of Park's relatives to take them there. They were dropped off by the roadside at a spot that they chose. They were told that they would have to find a ride home by themselves!

Park at 17, stocky built, 5'8" tall, he was wearing a soft felt cowboy hat. He wore Levi jeans and carried a large hunting knife in a leather case. He carried his camping blanket roll tied on to the bottom of a knapsack.

Joe was 17, 6'1" tall and thin and just 150 lbs. He was tanned and had a plentiful head of dark hair. He wore a straw cowboy hat. He wore a hunting knife in a case on his hip. And like Park, he carried a blanket roll tied to the bottom of a knapsack.

Joe said, "Before we set up camp we better get permission to camp on the farmer's land."

Park agreed with that. They went to the farmer's house together, to ask for permission. "Hello, Mr. Farmer. We'd like permission to camp on your property. Would it be ok?" Park asked.

"The answer is no. I have given permission to other people in the past and they have broken down my fences and built big fires that almost burned down my barn, so I won't let strangers use any part of my property. To use it without my permission is trespassing!" the farmer explained.

They said good-bye to the farmer and left. They stopped at the roadside and discussed what they should do next.

Park looked around and he noticed a stream of water that came down from the mountain. "Let's hike up this stream and look for a camping site." He said that they could walk in the water in the stream. "The stream is owned by the county, so we won't be trespassing on that farmer's land." Park told Joe.

"That's right!" said Joe, "Let's do it!"

Park led the way up the stream. Joe followed him, as they splashed through ankle deep, chilly water. As the stream meandered in several bends, after a half hour of walking, following the bends, the two were nowhere near the base of the mountain.

Joe spoke to Park, "Do you still think we will find a camp site by going this way? We are all wet from the water splashing on us. This water is becoming icy cold. Maybe we should try a different way to find a camp site!"

Park said, "Hang on just a little longer there has to be a good spot soon."

Joe answered Park, "Ok. I'll keep going for a little longer."

They both were happy that they went that little ways farther, because just around the next bend in the stream, they discovered a perfect place to make their camp. It was on a shelf like part of the stream's bank. It was high enough to keep the stream away from their campsite.

The ground was dry and covered with a thick layer of green grass. There was plenty of natural beauty all around them. The first thing they did was to start a small fire to use its heat to dry their wet clothes. They made the fire from dead, dry tree branches, called squaw wood. The fire would give off heat, but little or no smoke so its presence could not be easily detected. And the location of their camp could be kept from discovery.

Now they could enjoy their camping trip. Joe asked Park, "What are you going to cook for supper?"

Park said, "I'll be cooking something different, that you're going to like. It is woodchuck steaks. Once the woodchuck has been skinned, then the meat is bright red in color, like beef."

Joe said, "That sounds pretty good to me!"

Park took a break to watch a herd of white-tailed deer grazing in the meadow. "Come and see the deer, Joe." Park called to him.

Park came back to camp and cooked the steaks over the hot coals of the fire. When they were done, they both ate heartily. The woodchuck steak's meat was tender and tasty.

Then they went to their bedrolls for a needed sleep. The night was quiet and there was a sky full of bright stars over them. The night was an uneventful one for the sleeping Park, but Joe was still sleeping that next morning when he suddenly felt something licking his face. He was somewhat afraid to reach up to identify what was doing it. When he opened his eyes he was looking at the mystery licker and he saw a big, gorgeous Collie dog! It was friendly and loveable. He hugged the dog and played with it for a short time. That visit from the Collie dog was unbelievable, but pleasing to Joe. A short while later the dog left to go back to the meadow to resume his herding job of bringing in the sheep that were grazing there.

When Park woke up, Joe told him about the visit from the dog. He found it hard to believe and he said, "Joe, you must have been dreaming."

As Park and Joe were standing in their camp, they heard a rumbling sound coming from the meadow and suddenly the farmer appeared, standing on the bank above their camp. He had an angry look on his face.

He said, "I thought I told you boys that you could not camp on my land! Why are you here?"

Park said, "We aren't camping on your land. We're camping on County land."

"I don't know where you got your information, but I have owned this land for the past twenty years. All of the land, water and property rights are mine. So you are camping on my land, without permission, which is trespassing! So, you'll have to leave, right now!" the farmer said.

Park replied, "We will pack up now, and leave."

Joe was disappointed and angry but he started packing up to get ready to leave. He said to Park, "This has been a happy camping trip. I hope we will have many more together!"

"You know," said Park, "We aren't getting any younger!" With this declaration, Park stretched very hard. All that stretching made his ligaments and muscles sore, as they rebelled from all that strain.

Joe looked wide-eyed at the effects on Park from his stretching. He remarked, "Park, you sound as if you believe that we are getting old, come on, let's get going."

They knew that their ride to take them home was not coming. They decided to walk beside this highway all the way to route 5 & 20 at Toomey's Corners. On their way back they were optimistic about being able to reach it…at first.

"Boy, this is a beautiful day," Joe said. The temperature was in the mid-sixty's. They were used to walking, so they started walking with good cheer, but Joe was thinking, 'I don't think I'll be able to make it.'

Park got Joe by the arm and dragged him along. He made him keep walking even with his heart trouble. Finally, Park let him take a rest break, because he was having a hard time breathing.

"Look Joe, there it is, Toomey's Corners, not more than a football field's distance away." Park said.

Joe gasped and said, "Well, it's about time! I almost didn't make it."

They collapsed to the ground exhausted. They laid on the ground and rested.

While they rested they talked about how they would get the rest of their way home, to Canandaigua. Joe said that he had a friend who might come and get them. He went to the gas station and made a phone call to his friend, his Scoutmaster, who said he would come and get them.

"He's coming, Park!" Joe said.

The Scoutmaster, Dick, pulled up alongside of them in his truck. "Throw your gear in the back of the truck, and let's get going!" he said. They did, and Dick drove them to Canandaigua and then to their homes.

Park and Joe were best friends for many years and that camp out was the last one that they had together. Park lived out his life in Florida. Joe lived in New York State.

The End

THE FISHING STORY THAT I NEVER TOLD

By Joseph Beauchemin

In the state of New York, in a little suburb of Rochester called Irondequoit, there is a fishing spot at the start of Irondequoit Creek, just off the Southern shore of Lake Ontario that is only known to a few people. My son, Tim, is one of them and he and his wife, Rose, took me there to fish one day for Trout. Rainbow Trout there are respectable sizes. The Steelhead Trout there are fabulous and sometimes they are up to 30 inches or more long.

Tim hustled out and got ahead of Rose and I to fish. He had already caught a Rainbow Trout, when we got there. Tim checked with Rose to see if she was located where she'd like to be.

Rose said, "This is my favorite spot to fish from, but I'll share it with you, Dad.

Tim said, "Dad, take that spot next to Rose. She is sharing it with you. I'll set up a chair for you."

"Thanks Tim and Rose." I said.

Another fisherman came to the creek. He picked a spot next to mine. He never smiled or said a friendly hello. I think he wanted this fishing spot to be his alone.

Suddenly, I was on my back in icy water! "Somebody pushed me into this water! I'm gonna drown!"

"Tim and Rose, get me out of here!"

"What the heck are you doing in there? Don't worry Dad, you won't drown." Rose said. "How did you get in there, anyway?" Rose asked.

"I'll tell you about it later." I said. "Get me out of this creek, and please hurry!" I pleaded. "I'm not hurt, just wet and cold. Thanks for pulling me out!"

"What happened was that somebody pushed me in. Was that you, Rose? Of course it wasn't you. But, I think I know who it was! I'll have words with him later. Now let's get down to fishing."

So, the three of us settled down to fish! Our baited hooks were cast into the creek. But, Tim fished with a different method. He would cast out his favorite lure and then reel it back in and then do it again and again.

Then he caught a fish. I really wasn't paying much attention to them. My attention was really on that new fisherman, who bumped in to me and knocked me into the water. He never stopped to help. He just stood there smiling! That guy had the biggest stone face. He never even said hello. To myself I said, "He needs a lesson in manners!…And he'll get it from me!….later."

Then the stranger pulled out a steelhead trout. It must have been at least 24 inches long. It made a lot of splashing noise when it was caught. I went over to him to congratulate him for getting that big fish that he had just caught. He was still not friendly. I congratulated him again, but he still didn't speak, so I stared at him eye to eye and then asked him this question: "Did you realize that you pushed me into the water back there?" He turned quickly and said, "Yeah! So what?"

I kept staring straight at him, then I gave him a shove toward the water! He slid down the muddy bank and into the cold-water face down. As he got up and crawled up the creek bank, he had hatred in his eyes for me.

I quickly got right up to his face without flinching and said, "Now you and me have something in common, we are both baptized fishermen. Why can't we call things even between us?"

"Boy!" He gasped. "You are really something, you old fart. I admire your nerve! You know that you made me so mad that I could have killed you. Then you say why not call things even."

The fisherman extended his hand to shake on it.

Later on the way home in their car, Tim looked at me and said, "What possessed you to tangle with that big guy? He could have killed you."

"You know Tim, I'm kinda glad that he didn't." I said.

The End

A NIGHT IN THE LONG WINTER

By Joseph Beauchemin

This winter snow was plentiful, coming in heavy snowstorms and drifts piled up to the edge of the house roof. The temperature was in the 40's below zero. Never in my 18 years of living in these mountains, have I ever seen a wind chill factor as cold as this one this winter, being cold down to 60 below zero. I had volunteered to make a trial test of a new product, a tent that was made out of a new scientific material that claims to provide 70 degree warmth inside with outdoor cold down to 60 below. These tents, if they work, would be lifesavers for mountain climbers, exploders and all outdoorsmen.

I said to Jake, "If this tent is all that it's claimed to be then I won't need to bring a coat."

Jake said to me "You know Bob, I'd bring a coat if I were you. You never can tell what the temperature will actually be in that tent."

I entered the tent to start the test and snuggled up in my sleeping bag and settled down to spend the night as the trial test. I used my rolled up coat as a pillow. At first I was comfortably warm. The outside temperature was still fierce and with the wind chill, the outside temperature dropped to over 60 degrees below zero. In the first part of the night I was enjoying the camp-out, then the temperature in the tent dropped to way below zero. I was glad that Jake had insisted that I bring my coat. At the apex of the night the cold was almost unbearable. Then, almost unnoticed, the interior of the tent seemed to warm up. I removed my coat and just lightly used my sleeping bag. But just an hour later the cold returned and I snuggled into my coat again. It became unbearable inside the tent. Even though I was huddled in my coat again, I had had enough of the test and the tent. The trial test of the new tent was a failure. It didn't reduce the cold very much.

"Man! I'm gonna get out of here!" I exclaimed. I left the tent and sought out my warm bed in the house.

I stayed in there until I thawed out. "No more testing for me, that's for sure!"

The End

A DAY WITHOUT GLORY

By Joseph Beauchemin

Some days are better than others and some people are better than others, So Glory is like that too! In the 1800's the Union Army Cavalry earned justified Glory in battle in the Civil War. But, in that same historic period of time, that same cavalry massacred men, women and children at a place called Wounded Knee, a peaceful camp of Cheyenne Indians! In that there was no Glory. During those years the Army's policy regarding Indians was annihilation of them.

Can you imagine what it must have been like for those innocent people to have death rained down on them from uniformed men who just recently were their protectors! And what shame must have been in the hearts of those uniformed men, soldiers of the glorious U.S. Calvary! Orders are orders as all soldiers know. But that "Take No Prisoners" meant that their bullets were ending the lives of women and children in executing at command.

"There's one of them, Charlie! The first soldier called.

"You get him, and I'll get that fat one!" The second soldier said.

The Indians were running helter-skelter in an unaware panic. Rifle fire rang out continuously within the Indians camp. Women and children including babies were zeroed in the sights of the rifles. The Massacre was making some soldiers sick from the carnage!

"Just pile up the corpses." The sergeant ordered. "We'll burn them later!" He said.

This was a day that would be remembered....but a day without glory!

The End

THE INITIATION OF A MOUNTAIN MAN

By Joseph Beauchemin

Life in these Adirondack Mountains is pleasant, enjoyable and healthy because of the clean mountain air. To have a happy life and survive, residents of these mountains need to acquire knowledge of the mountain terrain, the climate and the temperature. To prepare the resident for all of these, they should complete the Rite of Initiation for a newcomer.

A longtime resident, Grandfather Smith has lived in these mountains for sixty years. His grandson, Davey Smith was getting extremely anxious for his turn for his personal initiation to come around.

"When will it be my turn grandfather?" he said.

His grandfather stared at him. He had a sour expression on his bearded old face. He said, "Now Davey, don't you go getting anxious about it. Remember that I am the mentor here, not you!"

Davey crawled up into the warm lap of his Grandfather. He always relished the strong grip his grandfather had. He felt protected and loved in those big hands. He held Davey so snug and warm.

Six months later when Davey was on his grandfather's lap again, his grandfather lifted him up off his lap and he set him down on the start of a mountain path that led to the top of the mountain.

His grandfather said to him, "I hope you are ready to begin your initiation that you have been wanting! Here is the first portion of it. All you have to do is to follow this path to the top of the mountain. Then find a spot where you can sit and gaze out over the beautiful mountain panorama." As Davey gazed out over the mountains, he marveled at the many different mountain peaks that they were all green and lush, with an almost uncountable amount of sparkling lakes and ponds. That fragrance from the evergreen trees wove a spell and sent love for these mountains through Davey's nostrils giving him a strong sense of belonging to the Adirondack Mountains.

Davey came back down to his grandfather, who said to Davey, "Now let's get on with the rest of your initiation. Go back up the mountain. Pay close attention to how the season changes completely."

Climbing up the mountain in winter was difficult. As Davey crossed over one slab of frozen river ice the ice cracked and he foot and leg went through and into the freezing water. He was lucky that his heavy snowsuit absorbed the water without harming him. And he was able to continue climbing the mountain.

Davey was icy cold all over and his face was covered with a thin layer of ice. The mountain panorama had drastically changed and everything was covered with white, cold snow.

When Davey came back down off the mountain again, he sought out his grandfather to tell him that he was experiencing stronger feelings of belonging and love for the Adirondacks. He felt that the mountains were more beautiful in the winter than they were in the summer. He was able to cope with the below zero weather.

While he was meeting with his grandfather, his grandfather told him about outsiders. "Every year a lot of outsiders come up to the mountains, from the cities, to enjoy friendships, sports and nature. They come up expecting mountain friendship and good old Adirondack hospitality." His grandfather continued saying, "Your next portion of your initiation will be for you to meet as many outsiders as you can, and to make one a good friend!"

Grandfather was pleased with Davey's progress. A wide smile spread across his face. He said, "Now it is time for you to complete this next portion of your initiation. Go back up to the top of the mountain, one more time. This time bring along a hundred foot long piece of rope. That would have been a help to you on the last climbs up this mountain. It must have been terrible difficult climbing up that steep cliff that's half way up. The rope will make scaling that cliff a lot easier. Also, bring along some of grandmother's canned preserves. They will impress outsiders and help in making friends."

Davey came back down off the mountain. With him was a young man his age. He introduced his companion to his grandfather as an outsider named Robert Brown. Brown was impressed with Davey's hospitality and friendship and his grandmother's preserves. He'd like to be adopted into an Adirondack family.

Davey stood, stretching to his full height, with his chest out full, as proudly as he could be. Davey said, "Those Mountains are very beautiful when they are covered with the winter snow and ice.

Davey pulled himself up to his full height and stuck his chest out proudly. He knew he could do it.

Grandpa beamed with pride and satisfaction over Davey's

successful completion of his initiation. He put his arms around Davey and told him, "Today you are an official mountain man and a proud addition to the Adirondack's seasoned mountain men!"

Grandpa and Davey are still up in those Adirondack Mountains. If you are ever up in the Adirondack's, why don't you look for them?

The End

A TALE OF TWO BOYHOODS

By Joseph Beauchemin

On an immensely bright, sun-bathed day, in a little town in New York, two young boys plotted to spend the day swimming in the local lake. The oldest boy knew how to swim, but the youngest one could barely dog paddle. Still, they both were determined to spend their day of freedom swimming and playing at the cool lake. They first had to walk the quarter mile distance to get to the lake. It made them hot and sweaty and their anxiety to get to the lake was getting unbearable. Their walking helped relieve the anxiety, but they still wished that they would reach the lake soon.

"I sure hope we're getting close to the lake, Bill. My legs are killing me." Dan, the youngest boy remarked.

Bill was the older boy, age twelve, athletic build, with long sandy hair. Dan, the youngest age 11, was skinny with a popular brush cut with blonde hair.

"Hang in there, Dan; I can smell the lake now. It just can't be far now." Bill told Dan that to encourage him to keep walking.

Not long after this conversation the boys turned around a bend in the path and they could see the lake. It looked crystal clear and was a pretty shade of blue-green color. The sun was reflecting off the surface, making mirage like images in the torrid air.

"Wow! Look at all that water!" Dan shouted as he saw the lake. He ran recklessly straight to the lake. He was wearing his swimsuit so he jumped into the lake, feet first, making a huge "cannonball" splash. He grinned happily.

Dan shouted, "Come on, Bill! The water temperature is perfect."

Bill said to Dan, "Remember, you don't know how to swim yet. Don't go too far out. Wait for me!" Bill shouted his worried reply.

When Bill reached the shore, he saw Dan rushing toward shore trying to get away from something out in the water. He was definitely afraid and had a look on his face that was as if he had just seen a ghost. It was definitely something in the lake.

Bill told Dan, "The water can't be that cold."

Dan kept pointing to something in the lake. "It came after me!" He cried. Then he kept rambling on, "There is a black, scary thing out there! It kept coming after me and it's still out there!"

A fearsome unidentifiable object kept advancing toward them until it reached the shore. Then it climbed up on the bank out of the lake. It then shook off the lake water. Bill and Dan were hiding in the bushes, watching the object as it approached the shore. They were relieved to see that it was only a buck deer with a group of lily pads entangled in its antlers. When the deer saw them crouched in the bushes, it dashed off towards the woods and was gone. The boys both laughed.

"Boy, I'm sure glad it was a deer and not a monster, like I thought it was." Dan said.

Both boys got a big chuckle about the incident. They went back into the lake and started swimming again.

"Stay in shallow water!" Bill Insisted. "You can't swim."

The lake was in a deserted area so they took off their swimsuits and went skinny-dipping. The water against their bare skin was relaxing. It was cool but not cold. After awhile they decided to lie on the grassy bank in the warm sunshine. The warmth of the sun made them sleepy and shortly they both fell asleep.

Bill was suddenly experiencing itching sensations on his backside. It was so severe that it woke him up. He rolled over on to his side to see what was causing it.

He shouted "Hey Dan! We've been sleeping on Poison Ivy!"

Dan responded "I knew we shouldn't have taken off our swim suits. Now what should we do? We'd better go back home and get Mom to fix us up."

Bill said "Let's get back into the lake where the cool water will ease the itching."

They got back into the lake and it did help a little. Then with only soft splashes in the still lake water, a rowboat with an old man out with his dog fishing appeared out of the sun's blinding glaze that had settled on the top of the lake water.

"Hey mister!" Shouted Bill. "We need some help!" As the boat came closer "Mister, we need some help!" He shouted again.

The old man rowed his boat up close to the boys and sa that they were naked. The dog barked a warning at them.

"Are you calling for help? What's going on? Why are you boys naked?" The old man questioned them suspiciously. Where are your suits?" the old timer asked.

They told him that they had left them on the bank when they went skinny-dipping. Then Bill told the old timer about the

Poison Ivy. The old timer made a knee slapping loud guffaw and almost fell out of the boat. He smiled with a toothless grin. Then he spit out his chew of tobacco.

"Say, ya fellas are in a real predicament ain't ya? I don't cotton to naked people riding in my boat. It's a bad influence on Skip, my dog."

"We'll be right back after we get our suits back on." They said.

Skip jumped out of the boat to join the boys. He stayed in the water, behind the boat, swimming alongside of the boys. The old man stayed in the boat rowing it along side Skip and the boys.

When they all met on the shore after the boys had put their swimsuits back on the old timer said to the boys, "My truck is parked on the dock, I'll meet ya there. Show me where you live and I will take ya right to ya house. Fishing has been lousy today, anyway."

"Gee. Thanks for the ride, mister." The boys said.

When they got to the dock, the old man was in the truck trying to start it up. The starter whirled a couple of times uselessly. He got out, steaming mad. He gave the old truck a few kicks. Then he got back into the truck and slammed the truck door shut very hard.

"This gull-darned thing needs a kick or two once't in a while. But it's been a good vehicle otherwise." The old timer said.

On the next try the engine caught and then it came alive with a loud roar. The boys climbed into the open back of the truck. Skip jumped in beside them. It was a breezy ride, but they enjoyed Skip's company. It was fun! Bill directed the old man to where they lived and he drove them directly home.

"So long." The old man said. "It's been nice to make ya acquaintance! Take care of ya itching ivy rash and stay away from Poison Ivy. From now on keep ya britches on!"

The End

PIERRE AND ROBERT FUR TRAPPERS IN THE 17TH CENTURY

By Joseph Beauchemin

Pierre LaPorte and Robert English, fur trappers, were following a trail through the Adirondack Mountains of the newly named state of New York. The time period was the beginning of the 17th century. Pierre was 6'3" and 275 pounds and very muscular, black hair, of French-Canadian decent. Robert was 5'8" and 190 pounds with blonde hair and of English decent. They met and became partners at a Mountain Man Rendezvous in Calgary, Canada. They were camped in the Onondaga-Iroquois village to trade with the Indians for their furs in exchange for trade goods. Some strange noise from the village aroused the trapper's curiosity. To observe the activity going on, they concealed themselves in bushes where they wouldn't be detected and could still see the activity.

The Indians brought in a captive enemy. Indians tied him to an upright post. Grass and sticks were piled onto his feet and legs and they burned the captive. The trappers experienced squeamish emotions from the devilish sight they had just witnessed. A second captive enemy was brought in. He too was stripped naked by the squaws who held him for running a gauntlet. They formed two opposing rows of Indians each carrying a club to beat the captive with. If the captive finished the run alive then he was given his freedom. This captive was beaten to death before he could finish the gauntlet run.

"*Sacre bleux, mon dieux,!*" *Pierre said to himself some choice swear words.*

"That's additional evil!" Robert exclaimed. "We've got to get out of this hell hole, and fast!"

They left the Onondaga village and had traveled only a few miles when they encountered two-dozen Indians sitting around a campfire. Both parties were surprised and taken off guard. The Indians jumped up quickly, hollering curses and threats and firing their muskets. Pierre returned fire and Robert did the same. They were both excellent shots polishing off half the Indian force. They were over powered and stripped naked and bound with a stick under their armpits and across their back.

Pierre said, "I hope they don't take us back to that Onondaga Indian village."

To his amazement, the Indians provided them with a canoe and let them go unharmed. According to a code these Indians followed, their freedom was given because of their respect for the trapper's courage, bravery and shooting skill. They kept their clothes and weapons. The two men quickly took control, stark naked, of the gift canoe just as the Indians released them.

The trappers rested and made a plan for getting to the Mohawk River by going south. When they reached it, there were two unguarded canoes beached on the riverbank.

"Take the biggest one and load our things in it and set it into the river quickly." Pierre told Robert. "Smash a hole in the bottom of the other one so they can't follow us." he added.

"So far, so good," said Robert, as they paddled several miles down river. "It looks like we have gotten way from those Indians. We haven't seen any Indians for quite a while. Come on you big Frenchman, paddle hard, if you don't want to get caught and roasted alive!"

Robert in anger said to Pierre, "I just can't stand it any longer, just to paddle while having to stare at your big and hairy ass."

Pierre had his say too," Well, paddling while having to stare at your skinny ass isn't my kind of thrill, believe me."

They decided to take another break. During the time of the break they stopped paddling, and they just let the canoe drift in the river current. Pierre leaned back and lit up his corncob pipe to enjoy his break. The smoke curled upward and was carried away on a strong breeze. Pierre grinned with satisfaction. From now on the pair would exchange paddling positions in the canoe. The compromise satisfied both men. Robert chose to use his break time to catch a few winks in a short nap

They had stopped paddling for a while and the canoe drifted freely, carried by the current's motion and it beached itself without either of the pair noticing where it had drifted. They were startled and amazed to find themselves where they had beached. They moved down the Mohawk in the naked condition that the Indians left them in. Their bodies were exposed to sunburn and insect bites. They needed a way to cover their naked bodies. At first they made and wore grass skirts. This worked for only a few miles. Then, as the grass got hot, itching became unbearable and the skirts were thrown overboard. The plus was there was no Poison Ivy in the grass.

They had traveled the length of the Mohawk River to Schenectady. They decided to search for clothes on clotheslines there in the town. From Pierre's search he found 2 trousers, 2 shirts and 2 pars of stockings. He also saw some lacy ladies things that he had never seen before, but they sure were interesting. Pierre didn't have the chance to verify sizes, but they looked like they'd fit. He brought the clothes back to Robert in the canoe.

Robert said to Pierre, "Well, it's about time you got back. Did you find some clothes?...Oh, thanks, Pierre."

The two trappers changed item by item until they found the item that fit, and they got dressed. They commented on how good it felt to have clothes on again. Their self-esteem was immediately restored.

Pierre and Robert began talking about their stolen furs. Pierre said, "I'm damned mad at those rotten Indians who kept our furs that took us over a year of work just to get."

Robert said, "I'm mad too. We should go find those Indians and get our furs back!"

Pierre said he had a good plan on how to get it done. "My plan will work, I'm sure of that!"

Robert narrated Pierre's plan to himself so he could memorize it. First get a few quarts of whiskey and give it to the Indians so they would get good and drunk. Then search the camp and find the furs, and take them back.

They got the whiskey and paddled up the Mohawk River searching for the Indians camp. When they found it the trappers drank their whiskey and, acted like drunken men, to entice the Indians to drink with them. The trappers acted like they were drunk. The Indians drank and did get very drunk.

Pierre said "Shay...(hiccup)...this here drinking ain't too bad! I'd like some more."

They searched the camp and found the furs and their clothes. Then they brought furs to their canoe. Then they changed from the clothesline clothes to their original clothes that the Indians had kept. That let them feel like their old selves. They could defend themselves again!

Pierre and Robert got in the canoe with their furs and weapons. Then they put the canoe in the water of the Mohawk River, and paddled into the swift water, happily paddling while singing old French trapper's songs. They dreamed of the profits they would have because of getting their furs back. They were anxious to get to the fur market in Schenectady!

Good fortune traveled with Pierre and Robert!

The End

A NIGHT IN THE EARLY AMERICAN WOODS

By Joseph Beauchemin

Jimmy knew it would be scary there in those woods that separated his village of Concord, where he lived with his grandfather, from the busy city of Lexington. There in Concord he earned the nickname of "Go-for", because he could do errands for people and accept responsibility for going after things for them, and bringing things back to them. Jimmy had accepted a "Go-for" assignment from the captain of the American Minutemen Army bivouacked there in Concord. His assignment was to get located in the woods, in secret, where he could keep watch on the stretch of the road from concord to Lexington. That's where the British were expected to make an invasion. He was to watch for any movement of British troops, then report to the captain immediately.

In Concord local people were calling the militia's soldiers Minutemen. They were prepared to fight with only a minute's notice. There had already been a skirmish between them and the Redcoats. The American Continental army was bivouacked just outside of Concord. In reality, what Jimmy was doing would make him an American spy. He didn't realize it then and he also didn't know that they shot spies, if they caught them.

Jimmy could see some British regular army troops with their prominent red coats making them great targets. They were making their bivouac camp in the meadow on the edge of the woods. He was hiding behind a large uprooted tree. It was a night without moonlight. The area inside the woods was extremely dark. Jimmy was becoming nervous about having so many British soldiers so close to his hiding place. He moved cautiously through the woods to find a safer spot.

After going only a short distance his progress was blocked by a British sentry who challenged him saying, "Halt! Who goes there? Advance and be identified, or I will shoot to kill!"

Jimmy stood still in the sentry's view with his hands held up over his head, in a gesture of surrender. He told the sentry, "Please Sir don't shoot me. I was just squirrel hunting in these woods. Look, here are two squirrels that I shot. I stayed too long. It got dark before I realized that it would be. I have been trying to find my way out of these woods, so I can go home."

The sentry listened to Jimmy's story and said, "Your story sounds innocent enough to me. However, I had better see what my captain makes of your story…after all, you might be a spy". Then he tied Jimmy's hands behind his back and blindfolded him.

"Give me that squirrel rifle, and follow me to the camp and the captain." He warned him that if he tried to get away he would shoot to kill. He also, said while bragging, "Pretty soon we British will be taking care of you Americans."

They both hiked off toward the British encampment, which was a few hundred yards away. They made their way through the woods. The sound of a musket shot echoed loudly though the woods. The sentry suddenly grabbed at his chest and then fell to the ground, dead! Jimmy was frightened by the shot and the sentry's death. He quickly sprawled out on the ground. He feared that there may be more shots coming…and for him.

An American soldier on a mission to locate Jimmy and bring him back came into the woods. He had shot the sentry. Then he helped Jimmy get up off the ground. He untied his hands and gave him his squirrel rifle. Together, he and the soldier worked their way out of the woods to where the lights of Concord were plainly visible. Then the soldier left to go on to another assignment.

Jimmy gave his report to the captain. "Sir from my hiding place in the woods, I saw a regiment of British soldiers setting up their bivouac camp. They had two 14 inch cannons and five 10 inch cannons. The British sentry who had captured me, was bragging saying, "Pretty soon we British will take care of you rebel Americans." He concluded his report.

That's nice work Jimmy, the captain said. "Your report will be very helpful for me as I formulate plans for the defense of Concord and Lexington."

Jimmy returned to his home. He was exhausted, but happy to be able to climb into his comfortable bed. Though he hoped to fall sound asleep, he was being disturbed by the screaming and moaning of men in mortal combat. He was finally awakened by the roaring sounds of cannon fire. He got out of bed and crept over to his bedroom window. He was just in time to see the beginning of the American Revolutionary War!

Jimmy stood looking out his bedroom window at the action. Suddenly, a stray bullet crashed through the glass of the bedroom window. He wasn't hurt. He knew that the window was not a safe place to watch the action from, so he went to the cellar to join his Parents and his grandfather, where they were hiding for safety and protection. He reminded his grandfather, "Like you predicted grandpa, these skirmishes have turned into a war."

The British, redcoats on the battlefield were formed in standing ranks in their traditional fighting positions, filing in volleys by command. They didn't take advantage of any cover or concealment, though they outnumbered the Americans at least 2 to 1. They were suffering more casualties.

By contrast the American minutemen took advantage of all available cover. They learned it from fighting Indians. The redcoats of the British made shooting them easy.

One thing he saw that made him sorry was the little British drummer boy fell dead in front of him. A bullet went through his drum, hitting him in the stomach. He couldn't have been more than twelve years old. It was so sad.

The battle raged on. The English king sent more troops to the colonies to put an end to the revolt and some troops joined this battle as reinforcements. This changed the course of the battle. The odds were 4 to 1 in favor of the British. Toward the end of the battle there were only about four-dozen American soldiers left alive on the battlefield. The British General compassionately offered to accept the Americans surrender. It was the best thing to do under the circumstances. An honorable surrender was negotiated and the battle ended, with the British as the victor!

Both sides exemplified high devotion and bravery. Even though this battle was lost, it showed the world America's dedication to liberty and freedom. They fought and persisted until they finally established and created a new and unique country, with freedom and liberty that has lived for over 200 years.

The End

THE DAY WITH A WOLVERINE

By Joseph Beauchemin

In the deep woods of the high peak mountains lives a creature that is feared and hated by animals and man. This creature is called a Wolverine. While it is no bigger than a large cat, it is as a ferocious evil monster seeking warm flesh and blood, unsuspecting bodies to kill or maim. It has instinctive foul body odor. It has been known to tear and render flesh and kill large animals such as a bear. Its foul body odor should be taken as a sign that one is in the vicinity. That would be the only opportunity one has to prepare a defense to protect themselves.

"OK Boys! Be on the alert. I can smell that rotten, Wolverine odor. It's very strong and I know that there is one in the immediate area. Quickly boys! Get into the truck and bring our dog Skip in with you. Keep all doors and windows closed."

The animal looked in our direction and then proceeded toward the truck, in a stealthy manner. As it got closer to the truck Skip was growling and barking. His wild climbing up the inside of the car door tying to get out and confront that animal. His wild pawing at the door caused it to come open. He hurried out and bravely contacted the animal, which turned out to be a Wolverine. Skip stood his ground bravely and at first had the wolverine on the run. Then it turned and came back at Skip ferociously. Its claws were tearing big hunks of flesh from Skip's body. It was certain from Skip's condition that he was in agony from his wounds. Bob grabbed his rifle and hurried from the truck. He took a shot at the Wolverine, but he was twisting his body and moving so swiftly that the bullet missed its mark. It had only just grazed it and did no real physical hurt. The Wolverine disappeared into the tall weeds on the edge of he woods.

Bob couldn't endure the sorrow of seeing Skip receive such terribly painful treatment from that monster-like, ugly creature. Bob felt that he had to put an end to Skip's pain and torment. He leveled his rifle to his shoulder and aimed at Skip's faithful head and with tears swelling up in his eyes, Bob fired the fatal shot that ended it for Skip.

He had been a faithful companion for him and his boys for over ten years. That thought raised the sorrow task of explaining to the boy just what happened to Skip and what to do about that Wolverine.

"Jimmy and Pete, I have some unpleasant news to tell you about." Bob said. "You saw Skip go after that Wolverine, trying to protect us. Well, that mean, bad animal was the worst thing he could have fought. It bit and tore Skip to pieces. He fought bravely, but he was hurt badly and was suffering. I just had to put him out of his suffering and shot him. Please understand that I felt so bad about having to do it."

"We sure do miss Skip!" said the boys through their crying and shedding tears. "We understand Bob!"

Bob and the boys continued on their truck ride. They went on the road that leads into the woods. After they had only got just a hundred yards in, the Wolverine crossed the road in front of them. It was moving swiftly and was headed into the woods. It paused shortly as the sound of the truck's motor attracted his attention. It recognized the truck and knew that the warm bodies of Bob and the boys were inside. Then it snuggled close to the ground and disappeared from sight. Bob stopped the truck and waited patiently, with his rifle at the ready, waiting for the wolverine to reappear again. However, the wolverine had a plan also, motivated by the thought of the warm bodies, meat and blood. It circled behind the truck. Then, disregarding Bob and his rifle, it climbed up on the hood of the truck and stared evilly through the windshield glass at the two boys with barred and foaming mouth, searching for a way to get in to them. Bob heard the commotion and reeled about to find the Wolverine standing on the trucks hood. He quickly spun the rifle up and focused the monster in his gun sights. Bang, bang, bang, his shots rang out. The Wolverine was caught by a broadside hammer of the three bullets. It was driven off the hood by the exchange of lead bullets and fell off the truck. It was frothing at the mouth and its eyes were blazing with anger and hatred.

As it fell to the ground, Bob rushed to the other side of he truck and bang, bang he shot two more bullets into the bleeding wolverine carcass. The wolverine exchanged one last dying breath. Then it lay in the roadway, stone dead.

Bob did his best to comfort the highly scared and fearful two boys. Then he started up the truck and quickly drove them all back through the moonlit night to the home camp. Fortunately, this was the only and last time that any of them ever saw, or wanted to see a Wolverine again.

Bob asked "Are there any other animals that you want to go search for?" The very loud and emphatic NO's were the answers!!

The End

A HIDDEN JEWEL DEEP IN THE ADIRONDACK MOUNTAINS

By Joseph Beauchemin

Up in this land of rivers, lakes and mountains, somewhere in those mountains is the hidden jewel. My friend Jake and I climbed up on that mountain and were trying to find it. Jake raised a question, "Why did our sources tell us that we could see the hidden jewel from the top of this mountain? It wasn't so!" We looked at each other with bewilderment and confusion on our faces.

I suggested that we browse around town and search through the local forests and bodies of water that can be seen from the top of this mountain. We may discover some evidence or clue to help us find the hidden jewel. Jake sided with me on that suggestion. "At least we would be taking some action. We might get lucky and find the true answer."

A short while later we arrived at the opposite shore, docked the boat and left it on shore. We both searched all around the town and especially in the jewelry stores. Our search resulted in no clues to the hidden jewel.

A torrent of rain interrupted our search and discouraged us. Then the storm expanded into a violent thunder-and-lightening storm. The clouds were throwing out bolts of lightning that were hitting the ground. We rushed to the boat, hoping to get shelter from the overturned boat. I made it safely, but Jake didn't. He was struck by one of those bolts. He was pretty shook up but not seriously hurt. He kept coming, crawling the last part of his way to the boat. He got under it and tried to settle down. Smoke drifted up out of his clothes.

We stayed under the boat. Our nerves were on edge from this experience. We were clinging to each other for support and for warmth. Under the circumstances we both felt it was best to go back to the lodge to rest and recover, so we put the boat back in the water, and crossed the lake.

Back at the lodge, Jake was reclining on the sofa. He seemed to be sound asleep. Jake was trying to recover from that lightning bolt strike and the shock of it on his nerves. Although he was snoring and appeared to be sleeping, his body language and the troubled look on his face, made me think he must be dreaming and reliving getting hit by a lightning bolt.

"Have a good night Jake." I told him.

Jake suddenly rolled over, and then sat up straight. "I saw something that was glittering from reflected sunlight. Did you see that too?" Jake said. "That was a waste of time going across the lake." I said, "Maybe not. I saw that reflecting sunlight from beyond those pines across the lake also. What we need to do is go back across the lake and search in and around those pine trees. I am confident that now we are on the right track for finding the hidden jewel."

Enthusiastically we took the boat back across the lake to where the pine tree thicket was. Jake searched the thicket part, and I searched the pine tree forest. The sun high in the afternoon sky was bright and its rays were clearly seen reflecting off of something beyond that pine forest.

"Do you see those reflections Jake?"

"Yes, I sure do!" Jake answered.

"I'm going to go through those pines to what is beyond them and find what those reflections are. Come and join me in this Jake," I said.

As we broke through that thicket and pine forest we came upon a very beautiful oval shaped pond. The water in the pond was reflecting the clear blue of the sky. The sunshine was glimmering like a hidden jewel.

"This is it Jake. Now we have answered the question where is this hidden jewel," I exclaimed.

"Wow, I can see that you're right! Hurrah for us!" Jake said.

The End

TWO BOYS AND A RAFT OF ADVENTURE

By Joseph Beauchemin

In middle of the summer, with a beautiful lake tantalizing them and building up an irrepressible desire to sail on the lake, two young local boys teamed up to build a dependable raft. Their dream was to have an exploring adventure, sailing on a raft on that beautiful lake. The oldest boy, Barney was 16 and 5'4", with thick, shiny black hair. He was very creative and artistic. The youngest boy, Joe was 15 and 6'1", with long, dark brown, wavy hair. He was also creative, smart and loyal to Barney. They got right to work creating and building the raft.

First they had to build the deck of the raft. "How big does it need to be?" Joe asked Barney.

Barney answered, "It should be at least 12'x12' with a movable sail at least 5' high and 4' wide." So they started building the deck from scrap lumber they found in the neighborhood.

Then, Barney explained the next step in its construction, saying, "We have to get four empty five gallon cooking oil cans, from some restaurant, to fasten to the bottom of the deck with strong wire and staples to keep the cans in place, to keep the deck floating on top of the water. The next thing needed is a mast for a sail and an old sheet to make the sail. Lastly we need a coil of strong rope the diameter of clothesline."

Joe said, "How are we going to get the raft to the lake?"

Barney answered, "We will put it up on two of the kids wagons and drag it down to the lake's inlet water where it comes into the lake, just before Squaw Island Bay. We will be sure that the raft floats before we take it on Canandaigua Lake!"

Once the raft was in the water they stowed their provisions of food and drinking water and jackets on board the raft. Then they climbed onto the deck. It had just enough room on board for the boys. Then they rigged up the sail. The wind off the water caught it and the raft sped along the water of the inlet at a fast pace and traveled out into the Squaw Island Bay part of the lake. It gave the boys great pride and satisfaction to see their creation, the raft, really float!

"Boy, Barney, this is going to be a great day of fun." Joe exclaimed.

Barney added, "That was just the beginning, wait until you see what I've got in mind for us!"

"What did you have in mind, Barney?", Joe asked.

Barney answered, "Today, we are taking the raft onto the lake." Right now, the surface of the lake's water looks like a sheet of glass. The sunshine was unusually hot and it beat down mercilessly on the small craft and its crew. The boys got sunburned and hot. It was hard for them to resist sliding over the edge of the raft and slip into the cool, refreshing lake water.

They sailed out of Squaw Island Bay and entered into Canandaigua Lake. Their course was to move toward Bare Hill of the Seneca Indians. They peered through the depths of water at the sandy lake bottom as they progressed. As the depths increased they began to be a bit scared. At noon, they got into their provisions for food and drinking water to quench their thirst. Barney had a sandwich and some drinking water, Joe had some of the water and sandwich also. Joe was satisfied with a couple of drinks of water, which was tepid by then. They stretched out on the deck to rest for a few minutes. Joe raised himself up to stretch and discovered white caps on the top of the waves. They were rocking the raft, causing it to pitch dangerously in a way that could possibly tip the raft over They made a nautical decision that it would be wise to change course and to steer the raft toward shore and prevent their becoming victims of a drowning tragedy. Barney adjusted the sail and headed toward shore at Roseland Park on the far side of the lake.

The wind and the white capped waves gave them some trouble; but the biggest danger came from the wakes of motorboats and one in particular, a Criss Craft boat that kept buzzing the raft, until it tipped over and dumped the boys into the chilly water. The boat sped off, leaving the boys bobbing up and down, treading water to stay afloat. They had no solid footing to help them get back on the raft, and the sail was still pushing it away from them. Barney finally got a foothold and was trying to take down the sail. He did after awhile. He helped Joe, and finally both boys made it back on board their raft.

"Wow! That sure was a scary experience, wasn't it, Barney?" Joe asked.

"It sure was, Joe!" Barney answered.

"Gee, Barney, the wind is tearing this raft apart I hope that we'll make it in to shore safely.", Joe said

Barney said, "Don't worry, Joe, we can see the lake bottom and it seems as if the water depth is decreasing." Joe said, "The only concern that I have is that I don't want to have any more experiences like that one."

Presently Joe sighted land! He was so anxious to land that he could hardly contain himself... The raft was approaching the Roseland shoreline, and people on the Roseland shore were taking notice of the on coming raft and sail. As it got closer, they waved and shouted hello and welcome. They were waving and smiling at the boy adventurers.

Barney noticed how strong the wind was this close to shore. He decided not to land at Roseland, but instead to continue on their voyage. "This wind is perfect for going on. We will stay in shallow water to the City pier, then back to the Squaw Island Bay, where we started. Then we can go back up the inlet and find a place to hide the raft. The cattails would be the best place to hide it. In the morning after we've rested, we can go back to the hiding place and retrieve it."

"O.K. That sounds like a wise plan," Joe said.

They sailed and navigated the raft into the cattails. Then they concealed the raft in the swamp's cattails.

All the fresh air and sunshine plus the emotional impact of their day's adventure had exhausted the boys. They returned to their home to get a restful night's sleep; and it came to them quickly!

The two boys, charged with new energy, met each other early next morning at the location in the cattails where they had hidden the raft.

"Barney!! It's gone!" Joe exclaimed excitedly. "Somebody must have seen us hide it, then stole it."

"What are we gonna do now?" Joe added.

Barney's response was, "Boy!, I hate that, I was planning on having another sailing day today." He breathed a heavy and mournful sigh. He gulped and then said, "There's nothing we can do about the raft now, but we can keep a look out on the lake and maybe we can catch the thief using it. Then maybe we could find a way to get it back."

"However," Barney added, "if we should spot the raft, we should arrange for a meeting with the thieves to negotiate its return to us. Then maybe we will be able to get it back." Barney finished speaking. Joe said, "who ever stole the raft isn't wasting anytime in trying it out," because just two days later, Joe spotted the raft, under full sail moving out into the deepest depths of the lake. Joe was worried about where it was headed because he saw the white capped waves building up out there; it seemed that the thieves were ignoring the danger they were encountering.

In the Canandaigua Daily Messenger newspaper the next day a news article and a picture of the raft appeared under the headline, TWO BOYS DROWN IN LAKE The story text told how the boys were sailing on a home built raft that capsized while sailing out in the middle of Canandaigua Lake. The two boys drowned before the Rescue Squad could get to them! The names are being withheld pending parents' notification.

The boys read this in the paper and they were gripped with chills of belated fear.

"Holy Cow! Barney, that might have happened to us!" Joe shouted.

"You're right, Joe, we were lucky!" Barney held Joe for comfort, as tears ran down both their cheeks.

"THERE BUT FOR THE MERCY OF GOD," both boys spoke the same thought at the same time.

The End

BUILDING A THREE STORY TREE HOUSE

By Joseph Beauchemin

In the 1940's when our families were under wartime conditions, most of the adult men were fighting WWII. That left us free, unsupervised and bored kids. We grouped together for social contact and play. Our group was called a gang. We were like a family. We spent many hours together. There was no television. We used our imaginations to entertain ourselves.

One day, we all decided to get together to build a tree house. We planned that it would be a unique one. We planned for it to have three floors. We selected a tall, wide oak tree for our base tree. We had members with talent, such as Bobby, our leader. We started by cutting down small trees to nail to a large limb of the base oak tree to make the first floor. It was 12 feet above the ground.

"Get your hammers boys, and some nails and get working." Bobby said. Bang...Bang...Bang, our hammers rang out! "Come on you guys, keep it up."

Then the noise of our many hammers could be echoed, bang, bang, bang, and the first floor became attached. Next, the boys worked to build the second and third floors. Next they attached those two floors.

"Don and Skip, you help Joe, and Leon, since you're the strongest, you lift the small trees up to the boys with hammers and nails." Finally, the first 3-story tree house was finished.

A used mattress was brought in and placed there on the first floor to use for camping. It was memorable to awake from camping way up there. It was good that nobody walked in their sleep. We used the second floor to store all our camping gear and other equipment. The third floor was left rustic and used mostly as an observation deck to watch animals and detect enemies, from sneaking up on us without our knowledge.

We all agreed that we just had to have a rope swing for our tree house. I was volunteered to climb 16 feet up in the tree to tie a rope for swinging. I was a good knot tier, and felt lucky, so I took the fastest and easiest way back down and that was to slide on the rope all the way to the ground, and I slid all the way down to the ground. I claimed the first swing on the rope. So, standing on a limb 12 feet up, I jumped and dropped about 3 feet before the rope stretched out, then tightened. That put me in a fast swing, that took my breath away then I was swept out gently to a stop on the ground.

"Wow! That's a good ride. It's scary, thrilling an exciting!" I declared. "Yes, that really was a great ride." I said! I wanted to do it again, but it was Don's turn to use the rope swing. He swept down gently to a stop on the ground.

Now Don can take turn to swing. He was waiting nervously on the first floor and he was a bit scared. He was determined to swing anyway. He gripped the rope securely and clenched his eyes and he jumped off. As the rope tightened, he flew through the air in the most exciting ride of his life. He kept screaming and shouting…"Wow!"

"Out of the way, Don! I'm next!" Skip said. He stood up on the first floor, took hold of the rope and jumped off. He went flying, like a bird, with a satisfying grin on his face, from the motion of the rope swing. He had that silly grin again as he gripped tightly to the rope. He was a little scared, but anxious to go. He hung on to the rope tightly. He had a great swing and then stopped slowly on the ground.

We had some rivals who were jealous of our gang and the fun we were having. They would see us coming and going in one location, and they discovered our gang and saw the fun we were having. They especially wanted to try our rope swing. Bobby offered to give them a turn.

"OK, who wants to be first? Have your money ready. It's only $1.00 A ride Bobby said." The rival paid to have a ride. He was highly anxious to go. He climbed up to the first floor and gripped the rope tightly. Then he was on the swing and was caught up by the exciting motion of it. His complexion paled but he tried to act nonchalant, but he never asked for more rides.

Bobby wondered whatever happened to those rival kids. I guess Bobby's talk of money made most of them change their minds. Before the summer ended, though, we were all friends.

After we built the tree house, we decided to modernize it. We collected wooden packing crates from stores. With these sheets of wood we made walls and a roof. Those made the house look to us like a mansion. We were envied by all the kids in our neighborhood.

Then September came and it was time for school to begin again. We had spent most of our summer vacation there at the tree house. Then our patterns of activity changed and we spent less time there at the tree house. Gradually the tree house deteriorated and over time we abandoned it.

Twenty years later, my memory of our tree house was still vivid and my curiosity to see the tree house prompted me to bring my three sons to the spot where the house was. They had heard me brag about the house and they wanted to see it. It was there that I spent most of my summer vacation that year. But alas, my beloved tree house had not faired well over time. The elements and vandals had really hurt it. The roof and wall boards had been removed by scavengers that took a big toll. The rope was just a frayed object; just hanging into space with no current purpose. Instead of showing them a great mansion, the tree house was a disastrous wreck. I had no brag that I could make for my son's admiration, so they were gracious and gave me respect by just standing by silently.

Somewhere, in my heart of memories, a great part mourns the demise of that unique, 3 story tree house mansion.

A TREE HOUSE POEM

By Joseph Beauchemin

A tree house I'll always remember was our mansion in the Oak tree,
And sharing that summer with good friends that be.
Having great fun swinging on a rope,
And those who wouldn't try it were a dope.,
Cause we flew with a flair, with pleasure and ease.
It made me grateful that God made Oak trees,
Where boys could build that house in a tree.
Where we spent that Summer with glee.

The End

CHAPTER TWO

Memories

CAMPING WITH DAD

By Joseph Beauchemin

It was about 1945-46 and our dad agreed to take my brother Ben and me swimming, fishing and camping at the point where the sucker brook ran into Canandaigua Lake. This was a well-known spot for catching bullhead fish He showed us a trick for catching frogs for their legs to eat as food. He would put a piece of red flannel on to a fish hook and tease the frog with it and snag the frog, catch it and cut off the legs and then fry them. They were great eating.

Dad packed our tent and all our camping gear into our little red wagon and pulled it along the banks of the brook and down to the lake. It was a hot day, so we started out by going swimming in the lake.

An island named Squaw Island was just off to our right, about 3 or 4 yards caught my attention. Dad told me the story of how it got its name. The Indians hid their squaws there when Sullivan's army came through.

Dad said we could actually walk out to it through the water. There is a natural sandbar bridge between the lakeshore and the island, with deep water on both sides. It was both exciting and scary walking on the sandbar but Dad being with us gave us the courage to try it. The three of us started the walk. Dad knew we couldn't swim very well yet, so he kept us close to him.

Walking on that sandbar made us feel as if we were walking on water with the waves splashing against our legs. It felt risky, but we made it to the island safely. After about a half hour of exploring the island, we started our return walk.

Coming back, the sunlight was reflecting off the top of the water with a blinding glare. I made it through half the way back, however the motion of waves generated by the rising wind was hypnotic to me and I stepped down and miss-stepped, and went off the edge of the sandbar and into the deep water that was over my heqad. Dad grabbed me and pulled me back to safety. I was glad that Dad is so strong and alert and I watched closely after that. I watched to find his secret for catching so many fish, bullheads and frogs. I watched Dad closely to discover his secret. He talked to the fish saying "Here Fishy, here fishy." Hey, it worked!

It was getting dark so Dad told us that it was time to go to the tent and get to sleep. But, tragedy occurred unexpectedly. Dad opened the tent flaps, and then jumped back with disgust on his face. There must have been at least a million mosquitoes ignited by dad's flashlight beam. His reaction was faster than lightning. He packed up all our gear back into the red wagon and pulled the wagon to the road. My brother and I did our best to help. He pulled the wagon back along the brook to the car and then he made a beeline for home. My brother and I did our best to keep up with his speedy pace! We have never forgotten that camping trip. Dad also enjoyed the adventure…up to the mosquitoes.

The End

GRANDMA ON HER CREEPERS

By Joseph Beauchemin

My little Grandma, only about 5' 2"and less than 100lbs. was always a hard worker and even though she was in her eighty's she is still attentive and dedicated to her present work. For several years she has gone down to the local Catholic Church where she does the janitorial work plus the cleaning and replacing all the votive candles for people to light and say a prayer.

"I see that you are hard at work, Amelia!" The Pastor spoke to her.

"Yes Father." Amelia replied. "I've run the vacuum already." Amelia told him.

"I've also moped the floors in the church!" She added.

"The Pastor advised her to "be careful when you leave and go home. It is very icy out there today." He told her.

Oh, you know father that I would never go out without my "creepers." She replied.

A small smile crossed father's face. He was remembering when he first asked her "what was a creeper?" She had a pair of ice grippers attached to her shoes, which she always called them "My creepers".

I am her grandson and I can testify that she always wears her "creepers". I often went with her to town for church during icy times. I watched her walk across the ice in her usual speedy pace. Her head held high and confident with unwavering faith in the effectiveness of her "creepers."

"Son." She said. "These here 'creepers' are great on ice. You ought to get you a pair!"

The End

REMEMBERING THE ISLAND FRUIT FARM

By Joseph Beauchemin

In the 1950's, there was a farm owned by Richard and Jackie that was called The Island Fruit Farm, located about three miles South-East of Phelps street extension. There's a road on the right that goes south for about a quarter of a mile into the farm and goes up to the big barn with a workshop attached. On the right, on a little knoll, is the residence home of the owners of the farm.

The farm got its name from its location on land that is between the two Canandaigua Lake Outlets. The first outlet is on the East side of the farm and the second outlet is on the West of the farm. An island is formed between these two outlets. These two outlets then merge into one body of water just about two hundred yards from the start of the entrance road to the farm. From where the two outlets merge together, this water flows continually northeast through several counties.

The farm has two kinds of fruit orchards. Cherries, are harvested in July, Apples are harvested in the Fall. The lands around the farm are wild and the areas are good habitats for a variety of game animals such as deer, rabbits, squirrel, pheasants, and ducks, and also fish from the outlets. Fishing at Canandaigua Lake, which is close to the farm can be done at will.

While walking through the orchard one day, I saw a mother Terrier dog with four puppies following behind her. She was teaching them to hunt mice for food. I reached down and picked up a puppy to keep for myself. I put it in my hunting coat pocket. As the day went on, I forgot about the dog until I got home and heard the pup crying to get out. I named it Pal, and he was a loyal, devoted dog for me for many years.

I made my own trail from my house on Beal Street in Canandaigua so I could come and go to the farm as I pleased and not be observed by anyone, because I hunted without a hunting license. First I started from my home and went to Jefferson Avenue. I crossed it and went through a grassy field to the railroad tracks. I'd follow the tracks to and across Phelps Street and go to the sand pit area. From there I'd go to the west side of the first outlet and cross over the outlet water on a fallen log, like a natural bridge. Then I'd enter the hardwood forest. There was a Great Horned Owl that nested there. Whenever I went through there the owl would drop down out of his nest and unfold his wings to fly, making a kind of snapping noise that scared me. Then he would glide silently through the woods where I was passing and it seemed that he was checking me out. I would exit the woods and enter the grassland and go up an incline to enter the farm through the cherry orchard.

I spent a lot of my adolescence years hunting and exploring these areas.

I was hunting rabbits in the grassland with my bow and arrows when a rabbit scooted swiftly away from me, surprising me so much that I didn't shoot a single arrow at it, and it got away. To be prepared for the next rabbit that scooted out, I would pretend one was scooting out and I practiced bringing the bow up, releasing an arrow to where the pretend rabbit would be. This paid off, because about one half hour after the pretending, a real Cottontail Rabbit scooted out of the grass and I instinctively released an arrow quick enough to hit it in the chest. It ran off and died. I put it in my hunting coat pocket and then forgot about it until I was home ready to skin it. It was full of fleas so I destroyed it.

At another time while hunting, I found the body of a big buck deer some hunter had shot and cut off the head, antlers and neck. He left the body to rot. I was sickened at the sight. I figured that the culprit was a poacher who was hunting illegally, or he wanted to make a mount of the deer.

Before I left the farm the last time, I saw some things that were different about the farm. Dick was not around. The barn was empty and still. The house appeared deserted. It occurred to me that maybe Dick and Jackie had sold the farm and some other party was running it. The orchards didn't seem to be in the normal shape that Dick would have kept them in.

The second outlet flows on the eastside of the farm. A company from NY City came to this outlet to trap carp fish and bring them to the city in water tank trucks for use in city restaurants. They dammed it up to raise the water, then they let the water out to flood the area alongside the farm. Then they closed the dam again and many carp fish were trapped in receding pools where many carp were lying dead in drying up pools. The smell from the dead fish was horrendous. Later they were covered over with lime to hasten their decay and end the smell.

In summary, the last time I went to the farm was in 1951, just before I left Canandaigua to move to Saranac Lake to graduate from high school there in 1952. I saw abandoned, rusty pieces of used construction equipment. At the end of that main road through the Apple orchard, fifty or more Apple trees were cut down and the roots and the sod was removed. Over two hundred yards of land was bulldozed clean. What a shame to destroy such beautiful natural resources.

I know that time and progress march along, but I will always remember the Island Fruit Farm. I've been happy to share my memories with you.

The End

REMEMBERING MR. PURPLE'S FARM LAND

By Joseph Beauchemin

My last visit to purple's farmland was in 1985. The occasion of this visit was to enroll in the Finger Lakes Community College in Canandaigua, and take some business courses. I chose this college because I wanted to see the land again after many years. My friend Park introduced me to the joys of Purple's farmland in October of 1948 when we camped overnight under the tall pine trees on this farm. We explored, hunted and camped and practically lived on that land from October 1948 to 1951, when Park went into the Army.

To get to Purple's farm I took my trail as follows: I started from my home on Beal Street in Canandaigua, NY. From there I would cross over Jefferson Avenue and through a large open field to the railroad tracks. Then follow the tracks across Phelps street extension.

From there I world go through the sand pit, all the way to the water of the first Canandaigua Lake outlet. At that point there was a big tree that had fallen and spanned the water like a bridge. I would cross on that natural bridge. Once across I would follow my path though the small hardwood trees. I would exit that woods and be in a meadow that bordered the island fruit farm. From there I would cross the farm and reach the second Canandaigua Lake outlet. Then I would cross the water on another tree, natural bridge, from the bank of the outlet. I Crossed over the land of the drive-in theatre and went up to the 5&20 highway. Then I would follow that highway West to the corner of Canandaigua's East Lake Road and then travel South for about a mile to where there was a small gravel pit on the left side, bordered by a small patch of hardwood trees. Finally, I would go through the woods and exit on the opposite side and come to Purple's farmland. I arrived across from the where the college library is. I was facing a field and hill. On that hill in 1948 there was a huge pile of abandoned wheat straws waste. We had a camp we made inside the straw pile until I accidentally burned it down with us inside. Thankfully no one was burned!

In 1948, the Purple property was a perfect place to go to see herds of white-tailed deer.

The patch of hardwood trees was the best spot in woods for hunting gray squirrels. The surrounding field was a habitat for those beautiful ring-necked pheasants. Lastly, on the huge rows of the fields and meadows were good spots to find woodchucks sunning themselves. They provided us with hours of hunting and shooting pleasure. I'd rather have things be still the way they were back in 1948.

I was happy to see how the buildings on the college campus fit into the nature around them.

The campus makes me feel happy and right at home. I was delighted to discover that the campus of the college was located in the spot where we used to camp. I have many good memories of those days, and have enjoyed being there again.

The End

SOME HAPPENINGS FROM MY LIFE

By Joseph Beauchemin

I have been thinking of some happenings from the seventy-five years of my life. This one is something that happened when I was just an infant. I was too young to have retained any memory of the incident. I heard of it from overhearing conversations between my parents. The subject they talked about was a fall that I had when I was just an infant, sometime between 1934 and 1935 when I was just beginning to crawl. Apparently, I had crawled away from the babysitter's attention and I fell off the front porch steps. I landed on my chest in a spot over my heart. A large welt and bruise developed there, so a doctor was called immediately.

While he was treating my chest wound, he announced a discovery that he had found that I had a serious heart murmur. Further, he said that I would probably not live to be twenty-one years old. They had never been advised by doctors in the past that I might have any heart murmur. The doctor told my parents that the medical description for my type of heart murmur was Leakage of the Heart. That was very shocking news to my parents. My father seemed to take the news the hardest, because at the time of the fall, he was babysitting me. He seemed to feel responsible. He felt he was to blame for me getting the murmur. Of course he wasn't. In fact he had nothing to do with it. My sister and brother were told of my condition and they were told to be careful that no horseplay, rugged enough to hurt me was allowed, because of my murmur. My sister went so far as to be a self-appointed protector of me. She even would physically beat up anyone who bullied me.

Personally, I was never aware of this pact to protect me. There often were times when I had incidents where I faced emotional and/or stressful situation such as competitive athletic sports. To protect myself, I had to learn how to cope with times when I felt there was a short supply of oxygenized blood for an adequate amount of air for breathing.

My main problems came when I refused to compromise the fact that there are times when I do not have the physical capabilities because of my murmur. Mostly, I live by my habits and my training from life to never give up or quit. All my life whenever doctors examine and listen to my heart murmur they get a puzzled look on their face because of the unique sound that it makes.

I knew that I was not physically capable of running in that race:

"I tried my best to make the coach understand that couldn't run in that race, because of my serious heart murmur, but he wouldn't listen to me. He scheduled me to start the beginning of the race. The other racers pressured me into doing it. Finally, I did run to start the relay race for the quarter mile. As I continued to run my vision got blurry. My ability to catch my breath was not adequate. In order to catch my breath, I had to stop and bend over. I had completed the first two hundred yards of the race. I tried to continue on, but my legs felt heavy and the best run I could muster was a weak, leg dragging type of running. I had run only a short ways more when breathing became agony again. I didn't quit, or think of dropping out. I was determined to keep on running. I became terrified from the worry that I might pass out, fall or even die, from the way my heart was pounding. I kept on running. The thundering footsteps of the other runners in the race had been heard sometime before they passed around and by me and had continued on to finish the race. I can't adequately describe how much inferior emotion that I felt over my un-athletic performance so far in this race. My only saving grace was that I didn't quit.

Finally, I reached the end of the track. I was utterly breathless and exhausted. Then I collapsed in a heap, to the ground. The coach had left a boy there to help me if I needed him. After my heart rate calmed down and I could breathe easier, the boy helped me to go to the gym to report to the coach.

The coach said, "Son, you were running at the peril of your life. It's hard to believe that you made it through that quarter mile, with a heart problem. Why didn't you tell me that you had a heart problem?"

I told him "I had tried to tell you, but you wouldn't listen to me.

The End

There's another experience that I'll never forget:
When I was about twelve and my brother Benny was about eleven, we went to the lake for swimming. At the time, I knew how to swim, but my brother didn't. Benny used to follow me

everywhere. He liked to think that he could do anything that I could do.

One time I dove off the diving board into the deep water at the front of the board. It was a deep, wide hole. As I was swimming underwater, going back to take another dive, a big cannonball type of splash occurred in the water above me. When I looked up I got a very unwelcome sight. Coming swiftly down through the water was my brother Benny. As he got to me I could see that he was terrified and afraid of drowning. In his panic he grabbed me and clung to my back. I couldn't swim to get off my back.

At first I managed to remain calm, but we were both thrashing around uselessly. I remember how strange it seemed that whenever I opened my mouth, underwater trying to get air that I didn't get any lake water in my mouth, or so it seemed.

A friend who was swimming nearby saw our plight and knew that we were drowning. He pulled us into shallow water where we could stand up and our heads were out of water. We could breathe air again. Hurrah! We were saved! I shouted! We all stayed friends for the rest of our lives....and Benny learned to be a good swimmer.

The End

In my fifty years of driving, I've had three accidents. This one is the most vivid of the three:

One morning I was going into Rochester headed for my work. I came in to the city on Monroe Avenue, behind a city transit bus. Suddenly, the bus veered into a bus stop to pick up a waiting passenger. The driver had almost gone past the stop. He made a quick move to go back. His sudden, quick maneuver caught me off guard, before we collided. The front of my first new car was severely damaged. The steering wheel took such an impact that it was bent into an inverted U shape. My hands were on it with my thumbs hooked in it. My thumb was torn loose from my hand and the white string of nerves was exposed. My right knee had the car key imbedded in it. My forehead hit the sun visor and split a four-inch gash in my forehead. It bled profusely and the whole front seat area was soaked with my blood. My suit and clothes were also soaked in it. Amazingly there were no fatalities! That was my first new car. I was paying on a loan for the next two years, and had to go without it and find other means for my transportation.

The End

You won't believe this next one:

Here is how I just missed being shot one day. I was camping with some Boy Scouts. I had my 30/30 lever-action rifle with me to sight it in, and was shooting it at targets. I told all the boys about gun safety, especially not to handle my rifle because it was fully loaded. But one disobedient scout let his curiosity get the best of him. He just had to check out the rifle. He lifted the rifle and when I saw him bring it up to his shoulder, I knew that he was going to pretend to shoot it, but it accidentally went off. I was glad that I saw the boy pick up the rifle and was lucky that I moved my position from where I had been sitting, because the bullet went whistling past my head, within inches of my head. My heart raced wildly from the fright. The scout was greatly upset and frightened too. I hope this taught him to leave guns alone.

The End

Now a story about my mother:
My mother told this story about when she was healed from Polio. She was born and lived in Mooers Forks, N.Y. Because of the Polio she was crippled and couldn't walk. Her father believed that girls didn't need an education, she never went to school and, though she was intelligent, she couldn't read and write.

While her father was at work, her parish priest said that he could help her get well and walk. She told me that her priest came and took her to Brother Andrew's Shrine in Vermont to ask for healing. Brother Andrew told her to come up to where he was and she would be healed. To reach him she had to crawl to him. Then he met with her and told her to get up and walk, and she did! Her crippled body was restored to health. She brought several religious items representing Brother Andrew's Shrine, which she treasured for the rest of her life. She was a very loving, gentle mother and she passed on to me a close relationship with God.

The End

FOR MORE STORIES SEE MY TWO PUBLISHED BOOKS BELOW:
"Up From Adversity" Publish America, Baltimore, MD; ISBN: 1-4241-6092-8
An Autobiography

JOE BEAUCHEMIN'S STORYTELLER TALES

"A Triad of My Literary Masterpieces" Publish America, Baltimore, MD;
ISBN: 1-60610-380-6 Songs-Poems-Stories

46 SHEPARD AVE

By Joseph Beauchemin

This address is in the small Adirondack Mountain town of Saranac Lake, NY. The house sits on a hill above the sidewalk. There are about ten rooms on the main first and second floors. In the attic on the third floor, there are two more rooms. Plus there is a stair down to a cellar. This house was once used as a curing cottage for tuberculosis patients. For this every room has an attached open air porch.

But the greatest thing about 46 Shepard Avenue was the people who lived there, when I did in 1951-1952. It was then that they shared their house with me. That gave me the ability to attend and graduate from high school in 1952 there in Saranac Lake. They always extended their best Adirondack hospitality and welcome to me and all who came to visit. This was the home of my aunt Deal (Della) and my uncle Phillip Willette and some of my cousins such as Hilda, who suggested that I come to Saranac to graduate high she became a good friend. Marceline taught me social graces and how to be a smooth dancer. Aunt Deal became my guardian and a second mother that year. Uncle Phil made great potatoes and his patient endurance in coping with his disability gained a valuable lesson that was used to cope with my disabilities in my life.

Then in an upstairs room my Grandma Gates and my Aunt Margaret Perry, both who were over seventy-five, shared that room and the bed. They both were very good to me and helped m feel at home.

As I look back at my year there in Saranac Lake I remember and count all the valuable experiences in my human development that I gained from being there! I recall all the happiness I gained from being there with all my relatives. The relationships, friendships, and the joy of being there in Saranac Lake my birthplace and the mountains will never be forgotten. All this is still fresh in my memory even though in 2010 it will be 58 years ago and then I will be 76 years old!

The End

DAD TAUGHT ME HOW TO DRIVE

By Joseph Beauchemin

Driving a car is scary. It takes some bravery, persistence and skill. Learning to drive will be made easier if the would be driver has a strong desire to drive. I reached eighteen and wanted to be able to drive. That too persistence and skill, and the determination to become a driver. It also helps if they are tired of having to walk everywhere or having someone take you wherever you want to go. It has been thought that 'They who drive a car move in a separate world!'

When I wanted to be able to drive, like others my age, my father agreed to teach me how. He drove me in his car to a long dirt road, with little or no traffic. His car was a 1948 Buick Sedan. It had a standard transmission. It was long and had powerful 8-cylinder engine that make it hard to control the gas, to creep slowly. And its length made it hard to parallel park. It takes practice to coordinate the clutch and the throttle to drive the car slowly. He took me in his car to a long dirt road with little or no traffic. Dad said, "It's time that you started your training."

The first lesson was to learn about the clutch, brake, and throttle. It took some time to master how to shift gears and let out the clutch while depressing down to give the engine gas. Actually, for some time I made the old Buick hop, skip down the road and hop like a bunny, but eventually I could drive down that dirt road and back.

Dad finally said "I think you are getting the hang of this driving business!"

"Can I drive alone?" I asked.

"Sure." He said. "Just as long as you stay on this dirt road."

"Boy, this driving alone is neat! I'm gaining a lot of confidence, and am losing my anxiety about handling the car for driving." I said.

Dad said "That's good, because now we are going into town to practice parking."

I drove off that dirt road and for the first time on to paved and lined roads. Dad was beside me in the car. Dad had previously made sure that I had memorized all the rules of the road. I had passed and received my Learner's Permit. I drove up to Main Street and Dad said that I would be learning how to parallel park a car. I didn't know what that meant, but I was sure that I was about t find out.

Dad had more surprises for me. He said "Drive over to Lafayette Street hill." So I did. Then he had me stop on the hill and told me to use the clutch and brake to bring the car perfectly still, without any rolling downhill. Well I tried it and was successful, though I know I was just lucky.

After that I said to Dad, "That was quite a surprise, even more than the parallel parking!" He smiled and his face showed a look of pride. He answered with "You did a good job. You're almost ready for the big day…The Driver's Test."

On the day of the driver's test the sky was clear and blue. The sun shone brightly on the town where the testing was held. I was healthy and in good spirits, confident, and not too nervous. Dad's car was running perfectly so as the tester instructed, I parked at the curb, waiting my turn. Dad sat in the back seat. The tester got in and told me to start up. Could you believe it, I couldn't get the G. D. thing started! The tester got out and went to test someone else. Now, I was nervous! Dad got out and lifted the hood and did something to get the car started. I kept it idling until my turn came again.

When the tester came back to the car, he was a little bit perturbed. He directed me to turn on Main Street and to parallel park. I parked satisfactorily, but when I pulled away from the curb traffic was coming that I had not noticed, or misjudged. He had me drive up the street in traffic. Then he had me drive to Lafayette Hill and he directed me to park on a hill, but I slipped on my footing on the clutch and throttle. It took me three attempts before I could do it and stay still on the hill.

The last part of the test was to turn left and go down Main Street but there was a little old lady trying to get cross through the traffic. Other cars were passing around her, but I stopped and allowed her to finish crossing safely. I think this gave me credits that overcame any errors. SO happily I received my driver's license.

The End

A VISIT TO PINE POND

By Joseph Beauchemin

In the beautiful Adirondack Mountains there is a lovely small town named Saranac Lake, where some young people decided to visit a spot called Pine Pond for a day's outing and a picnic. Bob Brown was the oldest, 6', black hair and from a family of outdoorsmen. Joe Smith, Bobby's best friend, was 5'9" with sandy hair, and was a follower. Jane Branch was of the local beauties, about 5' 8" with fiery red hair, and Barb Jones, was short in stature, 5' 3". She had a winning smile and lovely black hair and blue eyes. The four of them settled into the boat. Joe filled the gas tank and made sure their was an extra can of gas in the boat.

"What is the real color of this mountain water?" Barb asked. She said, "This water has a lot of iron content and so it looks brownish."

"Yes, but how come it looks so blue? Jane asked.

Barb explained, "The blue of the sky reflects off the water. That's what makes it look blue.

Joe asked Bob, "Is there anything I can do to help you with the boat?"

Bob said, "Not right now, thanks, but I will need some help later.

Bob started the boat's motor and then he navigated across Lake Flower and to the Lower Saranac Lake at the end of Lake Flower. Bob pointed to a spot on the far shore across the lake and steered the boat toward that spot. The girls were restless from not being able to talk, because of the noise of the motor.

"You gals please be patient. We are almost there," said Bob. The boat slid across the lake effortlessly. Then when it was a hundred yards away, Bob shut off the motor and the boat's momentum made it glide up to the shore and come to a stop.

"Now, Joe you can help me! I want to get the boat farther up on the bank of the shore to hide it." Bob said. "There have been vandals who steal things from boats that are left in the open. That's why I have to hide it!"

Joe went with Bob. The girls chatted together as they walked to the pond trail. Joe and Bob left the shore and went to where Jane and Barb were walking, to the start of the pond trail.

Bob and Jane held hands and waited for Joe and Barb to hold hands also, a little way in on the trail to Pine Pond. Bob and Jane walked to the pond. They were steady's, but Joe and Barb were just good friends together, still they held hands on this date. They all were enjoying each other's company.

The trail ran through a magnificent pine forest. They followed the trail to the white sand shore of a beautiful oval shaped, blue pond. Across the pond was the towering Ampersand Mountain. The sun on the sand was hot on their bare feet and the water in the pond was chilly when they waded in their bare feet. A blanket was spread on the sand to stay warm and to get a tan. They both were anxious to go in the water to swim.

"Will you make us a fire to cook the hot dogs on?" Barb asked Joe.

"Bob, will you please collect some wood for the fire and sharpened some sticks?" Joe asked.

After the fire had burnt down to red-hot coals, then they were ready to cook hot dogs on sharpened sticks.

Jane said, "This fire sure is hot.

Bob said, "The fire has to be hot in order to cook the hot dog all the way through."

Barb said, "I cooked eight dogs. That's two for each of us and I'll cook four more for extras."

They all ate until they were full. They all enjoyed the meal. The sun was hot on the gorgeous sand beach. A blanket was spread out on the sand and the foursome laid on the blanket sunning themselves and getting a tan. That lasted for only an hour then, because they were hot and sweaty, they decided to go swimming to cool off. The girls splashed and walked bare foot in the cool surf. It was refreshing and they were enjoying it. Then Joe decided to swim. He ran to the edge of the pond. Then he did a deep dive and then swam about 100 yards, underwater. He surfaced at the surf where the girls were walking. Joe played alligator and creped up to the girls, but he didn't frighten them. Bob pulled his favorite splash, a cannonball, that splashed water all over the girls. They weren't impressed or happy with either of the men.

There they were standing in the pond when a mama black bear with two cubs came out of the woods and headed for the pond. She and the cubs went directly to the pond to cool off from the scorching heat from the sun. They completely ignored the four humans and rolled and played in the pond like kids,

Joe laughed, then said, "I think those bear are skinny dipping, because when they went into the water they were bear." No one seemed to enjoy the joke except for Joe and so he sulked and came back into the pond to swim. He completely forgot about the bears in the water. But they suddenly remembered him. Then Bob went splashing around and the bears were very upset about him and growled at him for being in their pond, but he hollered loudly and they were afraid of the human voice and hustled out of there, and hurried back into the woods.

Now that the bears were gone the two couples could enjoy the pond...They swam together and that was refreshing. They swam the in that pond and romped in the water until they were exhausted Then they went back to the blanket again, but it was no longer warm in the sun. It had lowered into the West, and its warmth had diminished.

Bob said, "We had better be going back, so we aren't going back in the dark."

"I agree!" said Joe. "It has been a very enjoyable day. Don't you agree, girls?"

Jane said, "I'll never forget our day out. Barb, this is such a lovely place. I'd love to come back soon."

They hiked back through the woods to where they left their boat. Bob got it in the water, pointed so they could get in. He had the motor going. Bob navigated back over the same path they had come on. Then they went to the edge of Lake Flower. The motor started to sputter and cough, then it went completely dead. The only forward motion they had was from the motor stopping until the boat came to a halt. They were stranded in the middle of Lake Flower! Someone had stolen the spare gas. The girls were suffering anxiety attacks, though they didn't show signs of being afraid! Joe tried to think of a solution to being stranded.

Bob stayed cool and in charge. He said, "The water is warm and the shore isn't too far way for me to swim, so you folks sit still for awhile until I get back. It won't be long. The boat livery is in sight at the beginning of the lake, so everyone lean to the starboard until I get over and into the water. See you all later."

Bob was a good swimmer and they all had to have faith that he would return. Meanwhile, Joe suggested that they all sing songs or tell stories, until Bob got back.

Bob managed to swim the distance between the rowboat and the shore of Lake Flower. He climbed up the bank of the lake and then he ran toward the boat livery. He arrived at the livery, winded and tired. He told his story to the livery owner and he gave him another boat and gas. Bob got in the boat and raced to the location of the stranded boat.

Joe saw him coming and he told the girls and that helped to keep them calm. Bob pulled alongside the stranded boat. Bob handed Joe the can of gas and told him how to fill the gas tank. He told Joe how to start the motor, and instructed him how to run it and which way to go. So Joe took control of that boat and he brought the boat and the girls to the livery, with Bob arriving in the second boat.

This story has been told many times, but each time Joe is given the credit for saving the girls. But those of us in the know, know the truth…that Bob was the hero! Thanks Bob! We all are grateful for your courage!

The End

THE HIKE UP THE MOUNTAIN

By Joseph Beauchemin

On a sunny day in the Adirondack Mountains at Blue Mountain lake, Judy and I came upon a trail, that led to the summit of Blue Mountain. We wanted to see the beautiful panoramic view from the top of it. We had to follow the trail and climb the mountain. We both felt that we were in good enough physical shape for it.

"Let me go ahead to be sure we stay on the right trail." I said.

"Ok, but don't go too fast." Judy replied.

The first one hundred yards was fairly level before reaching a spot where the trail starts to go up an incline, but still not too steep.

"This isn't too hard a climb. I've been in great shape, so far!" I bragged.

"Well, I'm getting a little winded." Judy mentioned.

We stopped to take a brief rest. We had no reason to rush. The forest all around us was beautiful, with Fall colors starting to turn. They turn early at this height and climate. I saw a tree that I learned about as a boy. It is called Ironwood and is easy to recognize by the bulging vein-like eruptions on the bark.

"Well, now that we are rested we can continue to climb the mountain. This next section is going to be much steeper. Let's go a little slower!" I said. I took a big stretch to limber up my muscles and get them ready for the climb.

"Are you ready. Judy?" I asked.

"Yes! I feel much better now, lets go!" Judy said.

"I think if we bend our knees and push with our leg muscles it will be less tiring on us." I said.

We got to the end of that stretch and the trail seemed to disappear. There was a young couple coming down from the top and I asked them, "How much farther is it to the top?"

"Oh, you still have a long way to go to reach the top." they responded.

To me it felt like we had already climbed enough to be at the top, or close! "Well, the only thing to do, Judy, is to keep climbing." I told her.

The next portion of the trail was going to be very different from the others. In the first place, the trail was no longer apparent and in clear sight. One of the young couples showed me where to go next to get back on the trail. There was a wall of granite reaching up about six feet, with a slow stream of water flowing down the wall. That makes climbing it slippery. There are small branches growing over the water. This course of the trail discourages most hikers from going further. We decided to climb it. I had to stop in amazement at how well I was taking all this hard exercise and effort. It was only one year ago that I had open-heart surgery and my endurance was better than it has been for years. Climbing like this wasn't possible then.

From the granite wall the trail entered a grove of Jack Pine Trees. Suddenly a big Red Setter dog came running out of the bushes on the side of the trail. For a minute I thought it might be a bear! The dog belonged to the young couple, who had let the dog take a leash free walk.

"How are you doing with climbing the mountain, Judy?" I asked.

"I'm doing pretty good, my legs get a little tired, but I can make it. Are we close to the top? Judy asked.

After another five minutes we could see the fire ranger's tower on the summit. We shouted "Hurray!" We shouted some more and hugged each other in joy, just to share our success in reaching the summit. The tower looked pretty rickety to me. Judy, being lighter in weight, decided to test it while I cheered her on. She saw and took pictures of the maximum panoramic view of the majestic range of Adirondack Mountains. The view just took our breath away.

"You know, Judy, we had better start going back down. We sure don't want to be going down without daylight. That would be extremely dangerous! Joe said.

"Don't go down too fast, and watch where you are stepping." I said.

We arrived at the bottom safely, but Judy stepped down on some loose pebbles and twisted her ankle BADLY. She couldn't continue to walk out. I came to help her. I let her lean on me for support and sometimes I carried her.

Before I left the woods on the mountain I pulled a fungi growth of a tree and wrote message on it, and gave it to Judy for a memento of our mountain climb! She kept it as a treasure of our day together!

The End

THE CARROT CAKE STORY

By Joseph Beauchemin

This is a sweet story about Carrot Cake; at least it is to me. It all started in 1940, at age 6 years on February 24th in Saranac Lake, NY. While I was in school my mother was going to make me a special treat. When I got home from school I asked her if she had finished making my special treat.

She said, "Yes I have. It is on the table at your special place." So I hurried to the table to see what my special treat was. I was surprised and pleased to see a beautiful cake that was just my special size, only for me.

My mom said, "Taste the frosting. I think you will like it." I did, and it was Peanut Butter Frosting.

"Gee Mom, thanks a lot! It really tastes good!" It was a great surprise for my 6th birthday.

My family and me moved to Canandaigua and lived there for 36 years. I still remembered the taste of that Carrot Cake that Mama made. She made it from scratch because she couldn't read a recipe.

I went out with Jackie, a girl from Naples and when I met Bess, her mother she had just finished baking a Carrot Cake. I fell in love with the carrot cake and the mother too. I didn't forget the girl though.

Several times when I would come to their home to pick up Jackie, I had some good talks with Bess and got to know her husband, John who was a big man, 6 ft., 250 lb. State Trooper. He had a very friendly smile, a good sense of humor and always treated me well.

Several years later, while in college, Bess sent me a special Carrot Cake with Peanut Butter Frosting, but when I got sick and had to leave college, the cake ended up in the hands of my roommate, who said it was delicious. Bess made another cake and brought it to me from Naples to Canandaigua to make me feel better.

After Judy and I got married, I brought Judy to see Bess to get her Carrot Cake and Peanut Butter Frosting recipes. I never got to see Bess after that because she passed away. Judy baked the Carrot Cake and it became our family specialty. Our family members ask for it on their birthdays. Judy got pretty good at baking that cake and I had no choice but to keep her.

The End

CHAPTER THREE

Inspirational

THE HURRAH FOR THE RUSHVILLE CLINIC

By Joseph Beauchemin

Note: The names have been used to identify the characters!

Now, For A Scene From The Clinic:

In a little village in the Finger Lakes of New York there is a medical clinic that inspires faith and a big hurrah from its clients and staff. There are some good reasons for this acclaim. It's mostly because of its professionalism and effectiveness in its mission of providing medical and dental care for residents in the local area. Greater than that: the clinic has a competent staff of physicians, dentists, technicians, and employees. They are also very helpful and friendly from first visits to my return visits.

A Story In One Act

Entering the Rushville Health Center, my wife Judy and I made a stop at the reception desk. We were greeted and helped by a very courteous and friendly employee. Then Judy had a chance to talk to Lois and they exchanged cordial concerns about each of their families. We always like to meet her, with a friendly greeting for us every time we come in. Then Tammy came and brought us to her dental work area for my teeth cleaning. She was friendly and caring. Her professional performance put me right at ease. She helped me recline in the chair. I fell asleep at once. She cleaned my teeth. Then suggested I use a fluoride treatment, which I am doing. Then a lovely lady, I believe her name was Amy, helped Tammy get me in the proper angle for taking X-rays. After the X-rays, Dr. Terry did an exam of my teeth. I didn't know what those technical words meant, but she did a thorough job. She checked my broken tooth and said that I had two options, to pull it now or wait until it gives me trouble. I choose to wait. All of these people had a good sense of humor, which I appreciate, because humor makes me be at ease. Their great reception and welcome took away my anxiety. The people that we met at the clinic made us feel as if we were their most important clients. Keep up the great work!

From satisfied customers, Joe and Judy Beauchemin

The End

MY NEIGHBORS COMPASSIONATE ACT

By Joseph Beauchemin

The End In the middle of a raging snowstorm that had sleet adding misery to the weather conditions, I suddenly developed a severe case of Cellulitis in my leg and had spiked a high fever. I was in an emergency condition requiring an ambulance to get me out of my home and transport me to the local hospital in Penn Yan, NY. All of the roads and my driveway were covered by a foot of snow and ice.

The ambulance was called and the First Responder emergency person arrived and as he pulled into my driveway he got stuck and blocked it so the ambulance would not be able to get to my door. The responder got to me and immediately packed ice from the freezer around me, and then alerted the ambulance. Because of the unplowed roads the ambulance reported that they were having trouble making it up the steep Italy Hill.

The neighbor had just settled down in his bed. My wife, Judy called him to ask if he could plow and clear the driveway. Jim knew it had to be serious emergency so he got dressed and came right over. He moved the First Responder's car out of the driveway and plowed it plus he shoveled the entranceway (ramp) up to the house. Hearing that the ambulance was having trouble getting through the unplowed road, Jim drove to meet the ambulance and plowed the road in front of it as it came all the way up Italy Hill and over Italy Friend Road right up to my house and driveway.

My neighbors name is Jim. There was even more that he did. Jim kept clearing the road in front of the ambulance all the way to the hospital in Penn Yan, some 30 miles. I'll always be grateful to you, Jim. You are the most compassionate neighbor that I have ever had! It is comforting to know that you are here. God Bless You!

This incident happened just days before Christmas and I was kept in the hospital for five days. Good deeds like this one are what help us get through difficult times.

The End

A TREATISE
WORDS OF FAITH

REFERENCES: THE BIBLE—GENESIS AND JOHN 1

IN THE BEGINNING WAS GOD THE FATHER-JESUS, THE SON AND THE HOLY SPIRIT. THREE PERSONS IN JUST ONE GOD!
God the Father made man in His image and gave him a body and a soul. He declared that man was made from dust, and to dust he shall return.

He declared that whoever believes in Jesus as the Son of God and the Savior shall not be condemned nor perish, but he shall have everlasting life. And he that does not believe in Jesus as Savior shall be condemned already. He who believes that Jesus is Savior is saved by his faith, not by any works he might do because BEING BORN AGAIN IS A FREE GIFT FROM GOD HE BECOMES A CHILD OF GOD! HE INHERITS AND WILL LIVE FOREVER IN THE KINGDOM OF GOD!

THE FATHER SENT HIS SON, JESUS, INTO THE WORLD NOT TO CONDEMN THE WORLD, BUT RATHER THAT THE WORLD MIGHT BE SAVED BY HIM (JESUS)

Jesus said, "Most assuredly, unless one is born of water and the spirit he cannot enter the kingdom of God. That which is born of flesh is flesh. That which is born of spirit is like the wind that blows where it wishes and you cannot hear it or tell where it goes. So it is with everyone who is then born of the spirit. God made humans of body (Flesh) and Spirit (Soul) and in the Image of God. Spirit is spirit. of enter the kingdom of God again when the body dies what happens to it? The spirit leaves the body; it is interned in a grave and returns to dust. In the resurrection we are given a new spiritual body.

The meaning of being born again is to be born again of God; not of blood line or of the will or wish of any person; so that no one can claim the pride of doing it by their works. It is by salvation which is strictly a free gift of the love of God.

What happens when a person dies? At that time the spirit leaves the body and death occurs. Where does the spirit go? The spirit is like the wind and no-one can tell where it has gone to. I BELIEVE THAT IT RETURNS TO GOD! I think so, because Jesus told the good thief that he would be with Him in Paradise that day, and his spirit was there.

At death the body is interned in a grave were it returns to dust as GOD DECLARED. At the Resurrection we receive a new risen type body. Jesus told us he was the Way, Light, and Resurrection.

So, what is the true meaning of being born again? I BELIEVE IT IS THE RESSURECTION, WHEN WE ARE TRULY BORNN AGAIN. As Jesus said we must be to enter the kingdom of God (Heaven). SO IT IS WITH EVERYONE WHO IS BORN AGAIN OF THE SPIRIT OF GOD. As I understand what the meaning of born again!

The End

JOSEPH BEAUCHEMIN HISTORY

Joe was born with a heart defect and the doctor told his parents that he wouldn't live beyond 21 years of age. He turned 75 this year. In 1971 he had his aortic heart valve replaced after going into congestive heart failure. Just before the surgery (which was done in Burlington Vt.) his heart stopped. They had to do emergency surgery and he was told that he had very little chance of surviving. His wife prayed with a minister friend who was with her at the time. The surgeon came out to the family and called the successful operation a miracle! Joe's valve not only wasn't functioning at all but he also had an aneurysm above it that was about to burst. He would have died instantly if that had happened. The new valve was state of the art in 1971 but much later it was recalled as defective. It worked great for a long time but in 1992 Joe had a massive stroke (defect) that left him paralyzed on the left side and with many other problems. Then it was too late to replace the artificial valve. He still has it in place. A couple of years later he started having seizures that are the side effects of the brain damage from his stroke. He still has them from time to time. They are the local ones that only affect the left side of his body.
    In 1997 he had severe blockages in the arteries around the heart and had five by-passes (a CABG) done. WE NEARLY

JOSEPH BEAUCHEMIN

LOST HIM AGAIN. *His vein in his left leg was stripped to use for the by-pass and he has since (12 times so far) has been hospitalized with severe cellulitis infections for 4 to 5 days at a time.*

What we are dealing with now is called Brady-Tachy Syndrome with Atrial Flutter and Atrial Fibrillation. It simply means that his heart goes from beating too fast to bating too slow and not functioning right with it is skipping or just fluttering instead of beating properly. His heart was shocked to slow it down and that worked but now it is going too slow. He meets this week with an electrophysiologist at Strong Memorial Hospital in Rochester, NY to be evaluated for a special pacemaker that they might want to put in him. They have to decide if he can tolerate the procedure. He was able to tolerate the procedure and had the special pacemaker inserted in 2009. He is doing better but the pacemaker works most of the time for him.

Joe also has a small hole in his heart that doctors had never discovered before and it is very unusual. They decided he could not have it repaired without risking his life so he is living with that hole in his heart. He has a lot of trouble keeping his blood thinner under control too.

Joe is amazing in his faith and he keeps going in spite of his limitations. He gets around in a power chair and types stories on his computer using a pencil as a pointer. He has written and published two books and is completing a third book. All this was done since his stroke. He has been an inspiration to many other people who must live or recover from their handicaps or limitations. Surely the Lord has used him. His wonderful sense of humor is a gift from God and keeps all of us going.

Medical History

Joseph E. Beauchemin   DOB: 2/24/1934
Revised: June 2010
Rheumatic Heart Disease	1963
Mechanical Aortic Valve Replacement (Star if the East)	1971
Chronic Anticoagulation with Coumadin	
Embolic Right Hemispheric CVA	1992
Focal Seizure Disorder Secondary to CVA since	1994
Requires high therapeutic Dilantin levels	
Major Depression Disorder recurring since	1982
B-12 Deficiency since	1995
History of Peptic Ulcer Disease with Upper	
GI Hemorrhage	1994
BPH	1995
Benign Colonic Polyps	1995
CAD with Angina	1997
Presenting primarily as exertional dyspnea status post	
CABG	1997
Impingement in Right Shoulder	1998-99
Cellulitis Left Leg: 4/1997; 8/1999, 12/1999, 9/2001; 8/2002;	
9/2002, 5/2003; 3/2004; 7/2004; 12/2007; 6/2009	
Cellulitis Left Hand	11/1999
Cellulitis Right Hand	3/2006;
	12/2007
Requires SBE Prophylaxis d/t Mechanical Valve	
Fracture of Left Pelvis from a fall	9/2000
Laceration of Left Ear from a fall	
(Sutures and Tetanus Shot)	2/11/2001
Bronchitis	12/2001
Bradycardia since	1999
Brady-Tachy Syndrome with Atrial Flutter	1/2002
Cardioversion Shock	1/2002; 8/2009

JOSEPH BEAUCHEMIN

Cardiac Catherization		10/2003
Cataracts Removed—Both Eyes		2007
Peripheral Neuropathy		2007
Ventricular Septal Defect (not repaired)		2008
Atrial-Fibrillation and Tachycardia	since	3/2009
Congestive Heart Failure	since	3/2009
Gross Hematuria		3/2009
Cystoscopy		4/2009
Doppler Echo Cardiogram		6/2009
Dual Chamber Pacemaker		9/29/2009
Hypothyroidism		1/2010
Hearing Test Determined Hearing Loss in Right Ear		4/2010
HINI Vaccine		1/18/2010

Pneumonia Shot and Annual Flu Shots
Dental Surgery: Total of 8 Molars Extracted 2005
Tetanus Shot 1-19-2009

HER AFFECTIONATE SMILE

By Joseph Beauchemin

She always has it brightly on her face,
It radiates from her,
And brightens up all who see her
Though her troubles are many,
And are beyond her control,
That affectionate, warm smile,
Is always on display.
She inspires those who see her,
And I am especially moved,
Because she has caught my attention.
Carol is her name, Larry is her mate,
Thinking of her is my fate.
I'm proud of her,
And am glad that we are friends.

The End

OUR MEETING IN FAITH WITH FATHER EDISON

By Joseph Beauchemin

He came to visit,
With his pleasing personality,
And his shattering laugh.
He brought me the prayer for the sick,
And treated me to the Holy bread.
My soul is joyous,
And my body feels stronger and healed,
He shared with me "The peace of Christ",
With the most sincere words.
Father Edison, he said was his name,
And his demeanor will bring him fame.
He says he next is off to Rome,
Our time together was short in my home.
But, it was not in vain.
And hopefully we will meet again.
Go with love Father Ed,
May God bless you as He has said.

The End

THE TRAGIC FALL

By Joseph Beauchemin

A Fiction Story

Fellow construction workers of the Barbera Construction Company observed the tragic fall of the body of a fellow worker falling through space headed for the ground, three stories below from a scaffold connected to the side of the nearby office building.

Bob Piney an experienced worker of the Barbera Company had been installing siding on the side of a five-story office building in Rochester, NY. He was working off a scaffold positioned along the wall, three stories up on the side of the building. Bob had a heart condition that sometimes caused him to be dizzy and passing out at times. He was being treated with coumadin, a blood thinner.

One time Bob was walking along the scaffold. Suddenly he felt like instead of stepping on something solid, like the scaffold. He felt that he had stepped into empty space. Then he could feel a strong breeze created by his body falling through space. He didn't even give out a prayer for help for himself. His body continued to fall to the ground according to the law and speed of gravity. He unluckily landed in a pile of construction supplies. He lived, but sustained several major injuries among which were a ruptured spleen and a punctured abdomen. Fellow workers administered first aide and called for. E.M.T. Emergency Ambulance Services who rushed the victim, Bob, to the hospital. Bob was bleeding profusely from a punctured artery in his abdomen. Doctor's and nurses spent 2or 3 hours before getting the bleeding stopped. Bob was in unbearable pain and was pleading with the doctor to give him some pain relief medicine but the doctor told him he would have to wait until he got the bleeding under control.

During Bob's hospital ordeal, I was in the same hospital. In fact I was in the next semi-private bed in the same room as Bob. When Bob was leaving I asked him "Where do you live?"

He said, "I'm from Farmington, at 175 Bowerman Road."

"Well, it's a small world, I lived in Farmington, NY, for 15 years. At 195 Bowerman Road."

"Well that's a coincidence…we could have been neighbors! It sure is a small world! Good luck to you Bob!" I said.

The End

WHAT MAMA ALWAYS SAID

By Joseph Beauchemin

She was an important lady! When it came to independence, she was an example of it. When I was young, she was always the boss. To me she seemed very large, but as she grew older she became physically smaller. Even so, during that time she was still the boss. I respected that she was!

Later as I grew up she taught me some mature things. She said to me, "Keep your hair combed and always be well groomed! So I did!

I was embarrassed when she told me about women and sex. She said, "When you are old enough for sex, always treat women with respect. Always be looking for the right woman to become your wife! So I did!

At the end of her life she said to me, "Sonny, I want to go home! "So she did! She passed over to her heavenly home peacefully in her sleep, like she said that she wanted. I miss her loving care. I know too that she is important where she is!

The End

THE LIGHT OF FAITH

By Joseph Beauchemin

Sometimes it seems,
When all hope is gone,
And all your strength has flown.
Just when you are about to give up,
The light of your faith,
Brings Hope back to you again.
And happiness returns anew.
Depression from a stroke or sickness quickly flees
And happiness return's anew.
And the blessing of a loving God,
And health and strength
Becomes yours again!

*The Spirit of a person will sustain them in sickness
or troubles!*
We call upon you, O Lord,
A Merry Heart is good Medicine
"Do not be afraid, only believe and you will be made well!
(Proverbs 16:27)
"Your Faith has made you well!" (Luke 8:43)

AN EMERGENCY MOVE TO THE MOUNTAINS

By Joseph Beauchemin

Tuberculosis-TB, was a big killer of the young and the old, for years in the USA.

"Daddy, Bobby is choking again!" Mary exclaimed. Now he is coughing up blood. He has an active case of tuberculosis and now the number choking and coughing spells are increasing. If something is not done now he won't be with us much longer." Mary exclaimed.

Her father, George said "I want to take Bobby to Saranac Lake in the Adirondacks where there are TB treatment centers like Will Roger's Hospital and Trudeau Research Institute. Saranac Lake is 500 miles or more away. I've heard that there is a train that goes to Saranac Lake from Utica. We could take a bus to Syracuse and then catch that train going to Utica and from there, on to Saranac Lake. I'll make all necessary arrangements."

Later, George said, "I've made the arrangements and bought tickets for us all to go to Saranac Lake this Saturday. I know that you all will love it there. I'm excited and anxious to be there. I've arranged at the Will Roger's Hospital for Bobby to receive treatment for his tuberculosis."

That Saturday they all got on the bus for the ride to the Syracuse train station. The bus driver took them right to the train station and the railroad car of the Syracuse train. They boarded the train to take their railroad journey. The ride was peaceful and normal. They got seated and planned to enjoy a pleasant ride.

After the train had gotten about ten miles out from the Utica station, it came to an abrupt emergency stop. Later, three armed men entered their train car. They had guns they demanded that passengers give them all their money or they would be shot. One man did refuse and they quickly shot him dead. In the baggage car in another part of the train, other robbers with guns held up and killed two Government agents. They were assigned to guard the shipment of two million dollars worth of illegal drugs being shipped to the FBI in Washington DC. That was the real reason for blocking the tracks to stop the train. Once the robbers had the drugs, they left the train. All the passengers were greatly relieved to hear they had left. An undertaker was called to remove the three bodies.

A railroad crew removed the two large trees that the robbers had placed on the tracks to stop the train. Then the train continued toward its destination. The State Police apprehended the robbers an hour later.

George said, "I am so glad that none of you were hurt! Man! That was a scary experience. But, it's all over now. Let's get back to enjoying our train ride."

Martha said, "George, how can we keep going when you gave that robber all our money?"

George said. "I didn't give the robber all our money. I held back half of it."

Martha, concerned, responded "George, you might have been shot too! You were Brave, but foolish! I love you for it though." Bobby coughing, said, "You were great dad! I'm proud of you!"Mary stated, "Thanks to you Daddy, we can still take Bobby to that hospital in Saranac Lake."

The family all settled down and rested during the long ride to the mountains. They bought sandwiches for their lunch. Unfortunately they had to get peanut butter ones because of the money shortage.

They knew the ride to Saranac Lake would take a number of hours, so they passed the time by watching out the windows at the beautiful countryside and the magnificent Adirondack Mountains. George and Martha passed the time by reading.

Bobby said, "I can't wait to breathe that mountain air. I'm sure that I'm gonna like living in the mountains. Oh, look Dad there are three deer feeding on that hill on the side of the train."

"That's good, Bobby, because I've bought a house for us in Saranac Lake at 46 Sheppard Avenue. It's the same house where I lived with my aunt while going to high school there." George said.

They arrived at Saranac Lake at about 7:00pm. George registered them into the Saranac Hotel for a few days until he had Bobby entered in the Will Roger's Hospital. By then their house at Sheppard Ave should be ready so they can move in.

George got Bobby settled into the hospital. While the rest of the family waited for George to be advised when the house was ready for occupancy. Then he would move the family out of the hotel and into their new house.

Bobby's treatments at the hospital became a five Year stay. The fresh mountain air helped Bobby with his tuberculosis, but it didn't cure him. Advances in the TB treatment, like the new medicine that produced remarkable cures, was the thing that was the most effective in curing Bobby of all his TB symptoms. The use of this new medicine attributed to the closing of the will Roger's hospital.

The End

BOBBY AND GINNY

By Joseph Beauchemin

Black clouds blotted out the sun. Shortly a deluge of rainwater flooded the street where Ginny lived.

Ginny looked up into Bobby's rain soaked face. She spoke and her words warmed a spot in Bobby's heart. "I love you Bobby and I always have, since I was a little girl back in our home town of Oswagetche. Remember when you and your friend Ben wouldn't let me play in your sandbox with you, because I was just a girl."

"Yes Ginny, I remember that little blond girl with her pigtails and a face full of freckles who we wouldn't let join us in the sandbox. Back then, Ginny, I didn't know anything about girls, except that they giggled and screamed a lot. Now I know a lot more about girls. If I still had my sandbox, you would be the first one that I would ask to join me in play."

Bobby brushed the rain water from his face and gently bent his head down and his lips found hers and they joined in a lingering, loving kiss.

He spoke to her again, in a soft, gentle voice saying, Ginny you mean the world to me and my life would not be complete without you I love you dearly. I've always loved that freckled face blonde girl."

The rain had stopped, yet now Ginny's face was wet, but from happy tears and not from rain. They joined hands and strolled down the wet street where Ginny lived, stopping at her family's house just long enough to drop off her raincoat. Waiting there for her was Ben Brown, Bobby's best friend who also was in love with Ginny.

Ben's expression was one of joy, until he saw Ginny and Bobby holding hands like lovers. Then his countenance changed to hurt and then to anger!

"Ginny, how could you do this to me?" Ben asked.

Bobby glared at Ben saying, "Ben...what are you doing here?"

Ben said sharply, "I thought I was coming to see my girlfriend, now you make me wonder just whose girl, she is. What is the real story here anyway? Why are you holding hands with my girl?"

"You had better have a good explanation! Some best friend you are!"

Ben and Bobby had maintained a best friend relationship since they were five years old. Over the years they had both been loyal and true to each other. They thought nothing would ever be a problem between them. Now came this major obstacle to their friendship. They were both in love with the same girl!

Bobby and Ben got together for a serious, man-to-man, talk about the obstacle and Bobby said, "You know Ben that it's up to Ginny which of us she chooses don't you?"

Ben asked Bobby, "How did this happen to us, Bobby. I remember the beginning of Ginny and me dating; then, you weren't interested in girls and you went into the Army. Ginny and me were alone, and at first she was just another date, but she grew older; she blossomed into a beautiful woman and she set my hart on fire with desire for her. I love her . We have been going steady for the two years that you were away in the Army.! You know that she always wanted to be my girl. When I left for the Army she said that she would be waiting for me. I just got tied up in a job for the government and by the time I got back, she was with you! So, how should we settle this; by fighting? That sounds like a kind of crude way of handling it, though we could. The best way is for Ginny to choose one of us. Then the loser will have to live by her decision, even though we both love her. Then hopefully we can still be best friends, once this is resolved." Bobby breathed a deep sigh of relief that that was done.

    Meanwhile, Ginny was wrestling with the hard decision of whom she should choose. She talked to herself, weighing both sides of the issue. Her long harbored love for Bobby caused her to whisper to her self "It has always been Bobby that I've loved." Then she went directly to Ben, who was waiting anxiously for her on the sidewalk outside her mother's house. Ginny held Ben's hand and looked him in the eyes and slowly and softly said to him, "I've loved being with you, Ben, and have wished that my feelings were different. But my long time feelings for Bobby and my always wanting to someday be his wife has meant that my choice is Bobby, if he will still want me…, I'm sorry, I never meant to hurt you."

    Ben, deeply hurt and with tears flowing down his cheeks, walked off despondent. Ginny called to Ben saying, "Have you ever met my sister Nancy?" She showed him a picture of Nancy. She was a beautiful brunette of twenty who has the most captivating of blue eyes and a stunning figure.

    "No" I haven't. I sure would like to meet her though!"

    Ginny knew that Nancy was in the house. She brought Ben into the house and introduced him to Nancy. "Ben, this is my sister Nancy. Nancy, this is my friend Ben. He's a great guy and

I think that you two will have a lot in common. The two joined hands and then left the house to go for a walk in the park, and get acquainted.

Meanwhile, Ginny went to find Bobby. She found him pacing the sidewalk in front of her house. "Oh! Bobby, it's you I love! I have chosen, you! I hope that you still want me? You do, don't you, Bobby?"

Bobby's face got all smiles and his eyes sparkled, as if he had just seen an angel.

He sputtered then said, "Want you? That's all I've been thinking about while I was pounding this pavement and waiting for you. Yes, I love you, and can't wait until we can be together! What's going to happen to Ben...does he know?"

Ginny told him about Nancy and Ben, saying, "They seemed to get along fine, and he was happy."

Bobby and Ginny were married that spring. Ben was the best man and Nancy was the maid of honor, they bought Ginny's family home and they lived happily in their old town of Oswagetche.

The End

CHAPTER FOUR

Mystery

THE MYSTERY ON THE PENN YAN BLUFF

By Joseph Beauchemin and Conrad Tunney

On the Penn Yan Bluff something mysterious was happening; strange, unidentifiable sounds.

"Connie, you live on the bluff, have you heard or seen any strange things or happenings?" Joe said.

"Yes, I have. Last week on Thursday, I discovered some big footprints, bigger than any human footprint I've ever seen! There were several of them in the soft dirt around my house. Personally, I want an answer of who made them and what's going to be done about them."

Joe, Connie's friend, examined the prints and commented, "Boy Connie, they are certainly not human. The maker of those prints must weigh 300 pounds, and I'd say it has a height of nearly 7 feet. I've got some ideas about this and what made them."

At first Joe had kind of forgotten this incident until the next Thursday when Conrad and Joe were coming down the driveway at his house. It was getting dusk but visibility was still possible. There in front of them were three huge, grayish black objects that were walking back and forth in front of his house, along the shore of the lake. The water was warm enough for swimming and Joe believed that's why the objects were there.

"Connie, what do you think the objects are?"

"I don't really know, but they sure are creepy! Why did they pick my yard?" he asked.

"Well, they are timid and quiet, so I don't think they are any danger to you or your family." Joe said.

Then suddenly the objects ran around in plain sight. Then they just up and disappeared and they were gone." Connie said.

"Where did they go? How could that be?" Joe asked.

The next time Connie and Joe met they talked about the mysterious things that had been happening.

"There must be some explanation." Joe said.

"What do you think those big objects are?" Joe asked.

"Well, I don't really know, but I thought at first that they were bears." Connie answered. Bears can't just disappear, can they?" Connie asked.

"We'll just have to keep thinking of possibilities," said Joe. "Boy, this mystery thing is frustrating. What more can we do?"

And meanwhile, there have been more sightings in other parts of the bluff. Joe found the camp of the culprits that he thinks have been making all the sightings. He found capes and plywood footprints. So he hid in the bushes and waited until the culprits returned. Then he watched them prepare for another sighting. They were dressed in black sweat suits. Over that, they put on capes, the color of a Sasquatch. Just before they left the camp they took the wooden footprints with them. Joe could identify them if he ever saw them again. Joe hurried to Connie to tell him all that had happened.

"Boy, what a con game that is!" Connie said.

Joe said, "I think we'd better get the Sheriff to follow up on this.

The Sheriff arrived and Joe told him all about the mystery of the bluff.

"So you found their camp?" the Sheriff asked.

"Yes! It's not far away from here." Joe said.

"Let's go there and see what we can find!" the Sheriff said.

As they approached the camp, two men seemed to be in a hurry to move things out of the camp and into a truck. They didn't see the Sheriff coming.

"Just what do you have in the truck?" the Sheriff asked.

"Just our personal possessions, sir." one man answered.

The Sheriff checked the contents of the truck and found capes and wood footprints.

"You are under arrest." he said and put cuffs on them. Then he caught the other man as he was fleeing, and cuffed him also. Then he called for a Sheriff's car to picked up the two men and take them to jail.

Conrad said "What could those men hoped to gain from such an elaborate con?"

Joe said, "I have thought about it. It's got to be lake frontage. If people thought there were real Sasquatch on the Bluff and lake shore they might be afraid and sell out, leaving their property available for real estate con-men to try a scheme like this one.

"Well, Connie there it is. The 'Mystery on the Penn Yan Bluff' solved!" Joe said.

The End

ACCUSATION AND ACQUITAL

By Joseph Beauchemin

Bob Barnes is a fifty-year-old executive of the Red Ball Manufacturing Company in Rochester, N.Y. He started with the company in 1989 in the stock room as a clerk. Then he was promoted to Stock Control Department Manager, based on his experience, knowledge and devotion to the Red Ball Co. Then he advanced and was promoted to Vice-President Of Administration. He is a knowledgeable company employee and has held many key positions of trust within the company, over his twenty years of successful employment. He is well liked and respected by executives and employees. That is why everyone was so shocked by the rumor going around the company, that he had embezzled $50,000.00 of company money.

Bob immediately enlisted company auditors to do an audit of his department's cash receipts. He wanted answers to two pressing questions. First, who made the accusations? Second, what evidence do they have to prove the charges?

The answer to the first came quickly. It was filed with John White, President of the Red Ball Company, by Clarence Twittle, Senior Vice-President of the company, and Bob's boss. Bob decided to question Clarence, but before he saw

Clarence, he felt he should go see President White, who received the filed accusation. He was a fair man and had expressed his respect for Bob. It would be wise to have him on his team.

"Hello, Mary. Will you set me up for a meeting with President White for as soon as possible and call me back to let me know when it is scheduled for? Thank you!"

She checked Mr. White's calendar and asked him about Bob's request for a meeting. Then she called to tell Bob the time for the meeting. He was pleased and thanked her again.

Mr. White, even with his 80 some years, still had plenty of hair, even if it was white. His aurora was that of a jovial grandfather, but in reality he was a shrewd and highly successful businessman.

Bob was at Mr. White's office promptly. Even at 50 years old he was still athletic in his build and stature. When he entered Mr. White's office he was well groomed and fashionably dressed as befitted the V.P. of Administration at Red Ball. His broad Irish smile was contagious to employees. His personality was warm and friendly. These were some of the reasons why Mr. White promoted him To V.P. He picked him as a possible candidate for the next President of Red Ball.

"Good morning, John. How are all the family?" Bob said in greeting.

"Good morning, Bob. Everyone is fine thanks", Mr. White extended his hand to shake hands with Bob. Bob gave John a hearty handshake.

"Well Bob, now that you have the meeting that you wanted, what was it that you wanted to meet with me about?" John asked.

Bob answered, "John, you are aware, I'm sure, that there is an untrue rumor that I have embezzled $50,000.00 from the Red Ball Company cash receipts."

John cut in saying "I never did believe that you were guilty of the charge. I told Clarence the charge was unbelievable."

Bob added, "I am insulted and damned angry about this charge, John! It is untrue and the charge is all lies. These rumors have got to be stopped! I definitely did not embezzle money from Red Ball!"

John said, "I'll call him now and emphasize that I want him to come to my office, immediately. Mary, make that call now." She did, and Clarence said that he would be right over.

While they were waiting, Bob brought up the fact that he had hired an investigator to look into Clarence's background for any possible wrongdoing.

Then, the office door opened and Clarence Twittle entered. He was a little set aback to see Bob there, but he caught himself. Instead of speaking about his reaction, he gave a greeting to John and Bob. "Good morning, John. Good morning, Bob. What is going on?"

John said, "I asked you to come here so we could get some answers from you to clear up and put an end to the viscous rumors about the embezzlement charges against Bob. What can you tell me about those charges? What evidence did you have to justify making it? Tell us now…and tell the truth!"

Clarence wiggled and twisted and was obviously uneasy in his chair. The color in is face turned a little white as he cleared his throat and spoke. "There never was an embezzlement. I made up the charge and then passed the story around to the rumormongers in the company and it grew and spread after that. It got beyond my control to stop it." he finished his confession.

Bob said, "Clarence, why would you do that to me?"

"Bob, I have always admired you and your success with the company. With Mr. White getting on in age, it seemed possible that he would choose his successor to move up to the Presidency. Jealousy of you is a more truthful statement. I figured that with your better standing in the company, that I would need an edge to be able to compete with you for the Presidency. I'm sorry that I caused such turmoil over the embezzlement. I guess it was just my bad luck. It was a gamble but I lost!" Clarence said.

John spoke again, "Clarence, I am disappointed with you in this embezzlement action. Your gambling action against Bob shows me that you are still addicted to gambling, even after I've given you a chance to reform and show some integrity. I have made my decision. In June I will be eighty-five years old, and will retire. I have decided to choose Bob to take my place as President of the Red Ball Company. Further, for the period between now and June I'm making Bob, Senior Vice President."

Clarence was shocked and bitter about John's announcement! The pupils of his eyes dilated in a fixed stare. His jaw dropped several inches, as he opened his mouth to speak. "But John", he blurted out, "You can't do that!"

His statement was wrong and John just ignored Clarence's outburst.

Then John spoke again. "There will be no reprisals. There will be no other changes in job duties and no adjustments in wages, between now and June, when Bob takes command. Then he can make any changes, etc, that he sees necessary. This is an acquittal of the embezzlement charges. This is my last word on the subject...the case is closed!"

The End

THE STORY OF LONE EAGLE

By Joseph Beauchemin

In the old days, to the Indian, The Great Spirit was honored in all things! Each day and evening the Indian prayed to the Great Spirit that he would give the Indian courage, strength and help to find his name. To find it he had to endure physical suffering and meditate his place in life, and pray, asking to find s noble name! The boy did all that and while meditating he saw a beautiful eagle, soaring alone and graceful high up in the sky. He knew then that Lone Eagle was the name that he had been given. He received one Eagle feather for his hair, as a sign of his becoming a man. As he grew, he received other Eagle feathers for his bravery, as an honor to him. The feathers, which continued to accumulate, he had mounted in a war bonnet that was a symbol of his rank, as he became tribal chief!

In battle to show his bravery and frighten his enemy, he would drive a stake into the ground and then tie it to one leg so that he couldn't leave that spot until he won the battle or died. To show his courage, he would touch his enemy with
  A coup stick (A decorated stick with a feather dangling off one end) and claim coup before he harmed or killed the enemy!

JOE BEAUCHEMIN'S STORYTELLER TALES

The Great Spirit gave the Great Plains of America to the Indians. Great herds (millions) of buffalo were put roaming on the Great Plains for making the Indian's tipi home, his food and his tools. In the beginning of the 1800's the U.S. Army Calvary massacred helpless old men, women and children in cowardly attacks on sleeping villages.

The tipi was made of buffalo hide as a cover over thirteen lodge poles raised in a conical shape. The poles were arranged around a circle, which represented the circle of the world. The poles crossed in the front to hold the smoke flaps. The tipi always faced east. In the center of the tipi was a fire pit. Two other poles held up the smoke flaps, which could be adjusted to cover the front opening showing the tipi poles.

So Lone Eagle became chief of his Cherokee tribe. He gathered his warriors around him and laid out their battle plan for the upcoming encounter.

"Red Fox, I'll need you to be our scout and bring Standing Elk with you, for the eyes of two see more than the eyes of one." said Lone Eagle. He continued to say, "The Army Calvary will charge our village at top speed. They will be shooting with their pistols and slashing with their sabers. Many of our people will perish. Women, children and old men will have no protection. "So this is how we will fight them, said the chief. Half of our group will arm themselves with bows and arrows. Arrows will come in at angles that bullets can't get into. Line yourselves up in a line facing the charging enemy. Wait until horsemen are within two canoe lengths, then all archers at once release their arrows. Keep repeating the volume of arrows. From then on, guns that required reloading will not be effective at close range. From that point on, it will be hand-to-hand combat. This is when our tomahawks and knives will be the best weapons we can use.

A lot of dead fell on both sides, but in the middle of the fight the Army's bugle sounded recall. The Army limped back to their fort. They will come again, but that time they will show more respect for the Cherokee.

Lone Eagle was chief for many years and eventually his people received respect and shipments of food, medicine and clothing from the U.S. and Army. He passed away while staked out in battle. His tribe raised his body up on a platform in a sacred spot on tribal ground.

The End

A MOUNTAIN FAMILY'S TRAGEDY

By Joseph Beauchemin

It was the month of February filled with frigid wintry days. In the Adirondacks, trapping for furs from the wild animals for income was the occupation of many of the residents. Their workdays usually began early in the morning to go to their trap line and check the traps.

That's the way it was for Bobby and his father Jim. Jim shook Bobby when he heard the ringing of the alarm clock at 5:00 in the morning. They dressed and put snowshoes on, then headed for the trap line on the mountainside. The falling snow covered the traps, making them hard to find under the snow.

Bobby said "I'll tie a rope up from the cabin to the barn so Mom or Ollie won't lose their way, going to or from the barn while doing chores."

A big snowstorm was creeping in around them. The wind was howling fiercely. Waist high snow had already accumulated.

With the men gone for trapping, Sally, the mother, and Ollie, the young son, were left in the cabin alone. Sally had put extra logs in the stove to combat the 60 below zero cold outside.

Then she decided to do some baking of bread, cake and pies. All those logs generated excessive heat causing them to flare up in fire and one flaming log fell out of the stove and as it rolled across the floor, it started the floor of the cabin on fire. Because her concentration was on her baking, the fire went unnoticed at first. Smoke began to fill the room.

Ollie saw it happen and he called out an alarm to his mother, "Cabin is on fire! Then Sally saw the flames and her eyes widened in horror.

Sally didn't understand Ollie's alarm at first. By the time she understood and reacted about the fire, it was spreading rapidly.

She was deeply concerned for Ollie's safety. She ordered him, "Get your coat and snowshoes on and go directly to the barn. Use the safety rope line to get there. Cover yourself with the hay to stay warm. I'm coming too, as soon as I finish. I'll see you there after that."

Sally had to leave the burning cabin and leave all her delicious baked goods behind and make an emergency trip to the barn, but she kept a woeful eye on the progression of the fire. It was obvious that there was no way that she could put it out. The cabin kept burning until it was completely reduced to ashes. A column of white smoke rose up into the winter sky at the location where the cabin had stood. Ollie in the hay trembled from tension. Then Sally joined Ollie under the hay in the barn.

The snowstorm hovered all day over the whole area of the trap line. The men worked all day through terrible weather conditions. Temperatures varied from 40 to 60 below zero. A fierce wind kept the snow moving and built deep drifts of snow. They made it hard to locate their traps and retrieve their catches. The results from their traps were an unhappy, slim harvest. In the first two traps they only caught two snowshoe rabbits. Bobby saved them to use for a later meal. Two traps held mink, which were caught by just one leg and fought so fiercely that they had to be shot in order to remove them from the traps. In a different trap they caught a muskrat. The best catch was a lovely Silver Fox. Bobby planned to give this to his mother, to make something out of it. Then they checked all the rest of the traps. They were all empty, but most had been tripped. Jim reset them all again. The couple discussed their present situation and agreed, that with the weather being so severe and the harvest so disappointing, they would be wise to head for home and wait for another day when the weather was much better. So they checked and reset the traps, took down and packed up the tent, and carried away their animal catches. Then they started hiking on the homeward trail. They were worried about Sally and Ollie at home alone so they moved quickly.

The storm increased in wind and snow where the two men were walking. Now that they had taken the tent down they were exposed to the elements again. The homeward trail was tortuous on the men with the 60 below zero weather. After the first hour they were approaching their cabin. They were at a point in the trail where they usually were able to see their cabin but it was nowhere to be seen. All that could be seen was a white column of smoke rising up into the clear blue of the mountain sky.

"There's been a fire! Good God!" Jim's heart pounded. "God help Sally and Ollie!" Jim gasped.

Bobby shouted, "Boy, I hope they went into the barn!"

Finally Jim and Bobby arrived at the cabin. They were saddened, about the cabin fire, but were happy to see that the barn was standing untouched. Jim prayed that his Sally had *taken refuge away from the fire and gone into the barn, to be warm and safe.*

Jim's voice trembled as he inquired into the stillness of the barn, "Sally, Ollie are you in there?" His voice resounded like the barn was empty. He stepped into the barn.

At first no life could be seen in the dimly lighted barn then, some movement came from within the barn's interior as Saklly stepped into the barn.

Sally stepped into the light and spoke. "Oh Jim, I'm so glad that your back!" She hugged and kissed him, under a shower of female tears. His faith in God restored as he hugged Ollie and Sally.

Sally wrapped her arms around Jim, again. "Oh Jim, it was awful! The cabin just went up in smoke. I made sure to get Ollie out of harm's way. I'm sorry that I had to leave my baked goodies and bread behind in the fire. I'm sure glad that nobody was hurt."

"Well Sally, what happened anyway?" Jim asked.

"I don't really know. I think that the stove was too full of wood and it over heated. I was pre-occupied. Ollie saw a burning log roll out of the stove, and it caught the cabin on fire." Sally said.

Suddenly Bobby shouted a loud "Hey!" expression saying, "I'm hungry! Lets cook the rabbits."

He cleared off the barn's dirt floor and then he dug a pit for a fire and started a small fire for cooking. Then he skinned and cleaned the rabbits. He roasted them over the fire. They all ate the rabbits and satisfied their hunger.

The meal was tasty.

"I'm glad I kept them!" Bobby said.

Bobby called Sally to his side. "I've got a gift for you/ He gave her his Silver Fox .

She was excited and happy to get the gift. "Thank you. It's beautiful. I'll make lovely stole out of it."

They all discussed what their future might be, when Jim said, "I'd like to build a new cabin. I could use help from all of you." They were excited and willing to help.

That next week they began by cutting down trees for the logs to build it with. Thankfully the weather had improved and warmed to a pleasant temperature. It made building much quicker and easier. They used a horse with harness to drag the logs to the location for the new cabin. In just a few months the cabin was almost done, but there was just one more log to be cut. The cabin's ridgepole, a heavy long log. Jim was sawing down the tree he chose for it. His saw bit into the tree and then cut through the trunk. It twisted and stuck on the stump. It finally fell off and smashed Jim's head. It fell off and back toward Jim. It hit him on the side of his head, rendered him unconscious. He was just becoming conscious when the emergency squad arrived. He was rushed to the hospital. Doctor's diagnosis was a fracture of the skull. He would be unable to continue to work for a year.

Bobby stepped in to take his place in building the cabin. Bobby worked steadily on the finishing construction of the cabin. He spilt rails for a rustic fence for around the perimeter of the property. He had an accident while using an axe to cut and shape the rails. The axe slipped and hit his leg. It bled profusely for a short time. The accident, while using the axe, gave him a serious wound. He recovered quickly.

He celebrated his eighteenth birthday by joining the Marines. It was his lifetime goal. Then he reported to Paris Island for his Boot Camp training. He became part of Battalion C. He was stationed in Iraq. He earned several medals for his valor! Then he was killed in action there. He was given full

military honors and was interned in Arlington Cemetery.
   Ollie matured into a 6'2—250 lb, handsome man with curly black hair. In his youth he dreamed of becoming a Forest Ranger, but the life's path he followed made it impossible. He chose Petit Larceny and was imprisoned for five long years. With that, he paid his debt to society and has been striving to rebuild his good reputation.
   Jim and Sally lived in the new cabin. Then, one day Jim had a fatal stroke. Years later Sally met a widower whom she married. They sold the cabin to Ollie who lived there, happily, for years.
   Trapping is still done in the Adirondack's, but it's no longer the profitable activity it once was. The Adirondacks are an ideal place for sportsmen.

The End